Killer Condo

Georgia Adams

The LitChix LLC
Atlanta, Georgia

First printing

Cover: Carter Dunn, Atlanta
Back cover photograph: Sarah Browning, Atlanta

ISBN: 978-0-578-07173-251600

Published by: The LitChix LLC, Atlanta, Georgia

Publishing Support by:
Booklogix Publishing Services, Alpharetta, Georgia

Dedication

To our children:Callie, Sarah and Philip
Cameron and Carter
Jonathan

Georgia Adams
AKA

Karen Mc Colgan

Patricia Browning
Joann Dunn

Chapter 1

Jordan slammed the door and tossed her coat on Andrea's coffee table. "I hate this stupid Atlanta weather. Need heat in the morning and AC in the afternoon. It's February. It ought to be cold. In Jersey it's cold in February." Jordan's coat slid onto the floor. "Frigging coat."

"Jordan, you seem too upset for this to be about the weather," Andrea said.

"Shit, you're right." Jordan plopped into a chair. "It's Jim. I've had it. This is it. Get me a lawyer! I'm so tired of being in this marriage alone."

"Nice to see you too, Jordan."

"Andrea, I'm serious this time. What's wrong with you? Why are you jerking your head toward the sofa?"

In her best former Buckhead socialite voice she said, "Jordan, I have a guest. You remember Misti don't you? She was one of our first clients when we were just beginning to get the Women's Justice Center together."

Jordan tapped her acrylic nails on the arm of the chair. "Isn't Misti the pole dancer? Is that her?" Jordan pointed to the petite woman curled up in a blanket on Andrea's sofa. Only a small patch of satiny skin was visible, along with a regal head topped by extremely short blond hair.

Andrea rolled her eyes. "*Former* pole dancer, remember? She is planning on going to Vet Tech school."

Misti sniffed and then a torrent of tears began. She was saying something, but it was unintelligible.

Jordan frowned. "What's that Misti? Did you say something about a bowling bowl? That can't be right."

"Actually, it is," Andrea said. "It seems Misti was recently married to a gentleman who has turned up dead."

"Ellllvis," Misti sobbed.

"His name was Elvis?"

"No, no." Andrea said. "Her husband, who was then her boyfriend, whisked her off to Vegas ten days ago. Apparently he is, uh, was a high roller. Anyway, while they were there, they were married by a minister dressed as Elvis."

Jordan leaned forward. "How awful! I mean the part about him being dead. When did this happen?"

Andrea sat on the sofa next to Misti. "Just this morning. She got back from yoga..."

"Cccclosed," Misti wailed, through a handful of tissues.

"That's right," Andrea agreed. "Misti said her yoga studio was closed this morning. Something about an explosion. Police and fire trucks everywhere, t.v. trucks pulling up. It was total chaos, so Misti said she went back home and that's where the bowling ball comes in. Apparently, after she showered, she found her husband bashed in the head with her neon green bowling ball." Andrea picked up a tissue box and handed it to Misti, "and well, she jumped in her car and wound up over here."

"What did the police say? Did you call Jerry?" Jordan asked, reaching for her chapstick.

Andrea replied, "No, when she got here I called 911 and told them what happened, and that Misti would be here at my house."

Jordan almost shouted, "You mean the police are coming here, to your house, to talk to her? Here we go again. Did you talk to Jerry?" She got out her hairbrush. "I thought the LitChix were through with real life mysteries and were going to confine murders to our book club." Jordan glanced at Misti. "No offence, Misti."

Andrea frowned at Jordan. "You may be interested to hear who Misti was married to. Lew Cannon. Have you heard of him?"

"I don't think so...wait a minute." Jordan's voice dropped to a whisper. "Are you talking about 'Loose' Cannon? The in-town real estate maggot?"

Andrea frowned and nodded.

Ignoring Andrea, Jordan said, "Everyone knows that guy's slimy reputation. Just calling himself a developer gives the whole real estate industry a bad name. Giving out bad loans and foreclosing on unsuspecting lower income buyers. What a slime ball. Where do they live, Tuxedo Road?"

Andrea shook her head. "No. Misti and Lew own one of those new condos that used to be warehouses on Marietta Street."

"Marietta Street? You made it sound as if she lived just a short jog away." Jordan paused. "What are the cops going to think if she drove all the way over here to Grant Park? Andrea, do you have any perfume? Where are Cay and Trish?"

"They are in the kitchen making coffee and some breakfast for Misti."

"What about Mr. Chanel? He didn't bark when I came in."

Hearing his name, Mr. Chanel poked his wooly white head out from a fold in the blanket enveloping Misti. She hugged the little Maltipoo close for comfort, and he was content to stay on the sofa and snuggle.

At the sound of the doorbell, Mr. Chanel began to bark.

"I'll guess it's the cops," Jordan said, "You want me to get it in case it's Jerry?"

"Thanks, but I'll go." Before she opened the door, Andrea tucked her blond hair behind her ears and straightened her work shirt, an old habit from her former role as gracious lady of her former West Paces Ferry mansion, Chateau Soliel. She peered through the peephole. "Well, well, look who's here," she said, as she pulled the door open.

Detectives Jerry Bongiovanni and Helen Morrow strode into the great room. "And I thought I was through with the Litchix. At least from a cop's point of view." He studied Jordan's newly dyed red hair. Jordan's former blond curls paired with china blue eyes had given her an innocent look betrayed by a mouth that could peel paint. The red hair was a better indicator of her personality. "Color looks good on you, Red. Looks like you're a real Joisey tomato. So where is Missus Cannon?"

Misti raised her hand as if she were in school. "I didn't hurt Lew, I swear…" she began.

Andrea interrupted. "You might want to wait until you have a lawyer present before you talk with the detectives. Remember what I told you earlier?"

"Don't tell me you have already called Lanier Poole," Helen said.

"Why of course I have, Darlin'. That's something I learned from my own tribulations. Always speak to a lawyer first."

"So, in the meantime, how have things been going, Jerry?" Jordan wasn't losing any time. Giving her red curls a flirtatious toss, she asked, "Ready for some more eggplant parmesan?"

"Any time. You know I do love your eggplant parm."

Jordan moved closer to Jerry. Her short stature made Jerry look even taller. "Tell you what, Jerry. You bring a bottle of wine and I'll whip up something you won't be able to resist." She gave him a wink.

Helen gave Jerry a disapproving look. "Let's get back to the case, shall we."

The door bell rang again. "That might be Lanier now," Andrea said, heading to the door.

Lanier Poole paused for a moment on the threshold so his silver haired radiance could wash over his audience. "Where is the lady in distress? When Andrea said it was important, I dropped everything and came immediately."

"Bullshit," Jordan said to Bongiovanni, who laughed. Helen looked disgusted.

Lanier made an unswerving course to the couch, sat beside Misti and put his arm around her shoulder. "You poor lady. We should talk right now, before we go any further. Where can we be alone?"

"Why don't you talk in my office, Lanier?" Andrea suggested. "Misti, you just take that blanket with you, darlin', and stay wrapped up good."

"Cold?" Jordan asked.

"Naked," Andrea replied.

Chapter 2

Lanier immediately made himself at home, settling into Andrea's desk chair and pulling a pad of paper and a Mount Blanc pen out of his briefcase. Gesturing to the chair in front of the desk, he said, "Make yourself comfortable, Mrs. Cannon. May I call you Misti?"

"Yeah. Fine. Whatever."

"Call me Lanier. All of my clients do."

"I hope that's your name, then," Misti said, giving a nervous little laugh. "Just a joke. I guess that fell flat, didn't it? About your fee, Lanier. I don't know…"

"Not to worry, my dear. I believe Andrea wants the Women's Justice Center to handle that end of it."

"Oh, she is just a saint. She is too good. I don't know how I'll…" Misti teared up and pulled a tissue from the box on the desk.

"Now, now. Let's not start crying. Your situation is one of the main reasons Andrea created the Women's Justice Center. She understands all too well about women in trouble because they trusted the wrong man. Andrea was wrongly accused of murdering her husband in the fall." Lanier propped his elbows on the desk and leaned forward with a sympathetic look on his face. "Why don't you tell me what happened. Start at the beginning, when you got up this morning."

Misti blew her nose. "Well, for the record, I didn't kill my husband either. OK, I got up about seven. Lew was already dressed. I threw on some workout clothes. I go to an early hot yoga class. Lew told me he was headed out and he'd see me later." Lanier nodded encouragingly while taking notes on a yellow legal pad.

"I went down in the elevator and jogged the two blocks to the yoga studio. As I was coming up to it I saw people all over the place and cop cars and a fire truck – they were right in front, and a cop told me there had been an explosion. The front window was blown out. There was glass and broken furniture everywhere. The cop wasn't sure what happened but maybe the studio had a bad furnace or a gas leak or something. Anyway, he said it was closed until further notice."

Misti sat up straighter and frowned as if she were envisioning the scene. "I asked if anyone got hurt, but the cop didn't answer. Then, he told me I should step back in case there were any more explosions, which scared me even more, so I went back home and went straight to the shower." Misti sniffled and dabbed her eyes.

"You're doing fine, Misti," Lanier nodded. "What happened next?"

"OK. Anyway, I took a long shower for ten, maybe fifteen minutes. Then I went to my closet to find something to put on and that's when…"

"Keep going, Misti. You're being very brave."

"That's when I saw Lew. He was lying on the floor in front of the closet. The closet doors were open. He was on his back covered in blood. Oh my God, his head was all funny looking. I hardly recognized him," Misti's voice rose to a squeak, "and there was my neon green bowling ball lying next to him all smeared with blood. It was horrible. I turned and ran. Maybe I let out a scream; I don't remember.

"The next thing I knew, I was in my car headed over here. I don't even remember parking the car. I must have left my cell, which tells you how crazy I was because I never do that. Ever. And that's it. I've been here just like this until you and the cops got here."

"Tell me Misti, when you got dressed after your shower…"

"Dressed? I didn't get dressed. I ran out of that place buck naked. Andrea gave me this blanket."

"Oh." Lanier coughed. "Ah, well I see. Before you speak to the police, you might want to think about putting on some clothes. Maybe now."

"Yeah, yeah. Andrea said maybe I could find something in her closet to wear. I don't know. She dresses like Mother Theresa, compared to me, that is. I might feel funny."

"Funnier than…Never mind," Lanier said.

Misti went into Andrea's closet through the connecting door. She soon came out wearing a pink lingerie-type top under a lacey black sweater and a pair of jeans, rolled up. "Andrea's a lot taller than I am, but I can work with these," Misti said. She pulled the blanket back around her muscular shoulders and sat back in the same chair.

Lanier tried to avoid staring appreciatively at Misti's petite curvacious figure. She radiated sexuality. He cleared his throat. "Misti, was there any indication someone had been in your condo while you were out or was still there hiding?"

"No, I didn't notice anything out of place, but I was so freaked out by that fuc…pardon me, by that explosion I could have missed it."

"Was the door to your closet open when you left to go to the studio?"

Misti frowned. "No, it was not. I keep things straight and Lew is very neat. Those doors were definitely closed."

"Did you notice whether they were open or closed when you got back, before you took your shower?"

"No, I rushed straight into the bathroom. I see what you are getting at. Lew must have heard the sirens and come back to make sure I was OK." Misti's hands flew to her mouth. "Oh, my God, this is so creepy. You think somebody came in and killed Lew while I was in the shower? They could have killed me too. I escaped death twice already this morning; I must have a guardian angel or something."

"I don't have any theories yet. I want to find out everything you saw and heard. You tell me everything, but tell the police as little as possible, understand? Never talk to them without me. Just answer their questions and don't volunteer anything else." Lanier jotted some more notes on his pad. "Oh, and skip the nudity part. That is, well, distracting. Now, can you think of anything that would have scared an intruder away?"

"Not really. Wait. There were a lot of sirens. I guess the cops and the fire engine came barreling down my street from the yoga thing. Maybe an ambulance, too. That could have done it. Scared the guy away, I mean. "

Lanier looked over his notes. "Misti, let's talk more about your bowling ball."

"Balls. I have four: the green neon I found next to poor Lew, a pink one that glows in the dark, a swirly yellow one, and a red, white and blue one, like the flag."

"Got it, like the flag. I take it you bowl quite a lot then, am I right?"

"No, not so much. About once a month with the Sisters of Piety over in Stone Mountain. We're in the Betsy Ross Bowling League. I know it's awful far to go to bowl, but the Sisters were so good to me when I was little, after my momma ran off."

Lanier cleared his throat. "We can come back to bowling. Moving on to Lew. What about enemies? Is there anyone who might have wanted him dead?"

"I didn't know any of Lew's enemies or friends. Not that his friends would have wanted him dead. Lew never talked business or told me anything about his past life. There was one odd thing, though. Lew was wearing a toupee when I …found him. I'm sure he was. He never did that. He had skimpy white hair, almost bald, and he liked it that way. I think the way he looked was sort of what pulled us together. People stared at him and they stared at me too." Misti sighed. "I called him my bunny boy 'cause he was so pale. Even his eyes were almost colorless. We understood what it was like to be different from everyone else." She took a handful of tissues and pressed them to her eyes. "Maybe he thought I'd like the toupee and wanted to surprise me. I'll never know. Oh, and there were a pair of broken glasses, which was odd since Lew wore contacts."

"Got it. You don't know if he had any specific enemies. Maybe someone with whom he did business?" Lanier prompted.

"Enemies? Lew never talked about having enemies. He was jumpy sometimes, but I didn't think anything about it. I never saw him with anyone else. A lot of men come to the club with other guys, but not Lew. In fact he didn't even watch the other girls. Only me. When I wasn't on, he just sat there with his crosswords. That was his only hobby, I think. He did crosswords and those other puzzles; they're called acc…acc..."

"Acrostics?" Lanier asked.

"Yeah, I think that was it. Anyway, he did really hard ones. His mind just worked that way. He tried to get me interested, but I wasn't much for it. As for enemies, he never told me much of anything about his life before he met me." Misti shook her head. "He said he wasn't too happy and that meeting me was like being born again."

11

Misti smiled at the memory. "He was a real big tipper, but I didn't pay him much attention. We weren't supposed to date customers, but after awhile he kind of wore me down, and we started going out when I got off work."

"And you were what at this club? A waitress?"

"Oh no. I was an 'artiste'." She lifted her chin. "A pole dancer. Nobody better. It's all in the upper body strength, you know what I mean? Look at these muscles." Misti flexed her impressive biceps. "Most men don't have biceps like this. If you don't have good upper body strength, let me tell you swinging on that pole can be dangerous. There are a lot of injuries in the business."

"I can imagine." Lanier tried not to stare. "Ahh, and you were saying you started seeing Lew after hours."

"That's right. He always had a bottle of expensive vodka with him. He liked Russian vodka the best. Anyway, we'd talk for hours, and then he'd drop me off at my place and I wouldn't see or hear from him for a few nights, and then there he'd be, back in the front row, stuffing hundreds in my G-string. He was so romantic."

"Sounds like he was quite a guy."

Chapter 3

"So, Detectives, looks as if Misti and Lanier are going to talk all day," Jordan smiled at Bongiovanni. "Jerry, you might as well make yourself comfortable. You too," she said, with a cursory nod to Detective Helen Morrow, who had been silent and mostly ignored.

Andrea stood. "Jordan, not to be inhospitable, but the detectives can entertain themselves. I need you to join Cay, Trish and me in the kitchen. Now."

"Aw, Andrea," Jordan whined like a child, "I want…"

"Jordan, now. You can talk to the detective later." Andrea took Jordan's arm and marched down the hall past the dining room and into her old-fashioned kitchen.

"Hello Darling," said Trish as she gave Jordan a big hug. "Can you believe what is going on here? I am so worried about Misti. What a horrible situation she's in. Would you like a cup of coffee? I just made it."

"Hey, Jordan," called out Cay. "Fill us in with the details. What is going on out there?"

Jordan plopped on a kitchen stool. "Misti and Lanier are busy conferring in Andrea's office and Andrea wouldn't let me talk to Jerry. Oh, Helen Morrow's here too."

Andrea poured a cup of coffee and handed it to Jordan. She turned to Cay and Trish. "Did either of you recognize Misti's husband's name, Lew Cannon?"

Cay and Trish looked at one another. Cay shrugged. "It doesn't ring a bell with me."

"Me, either. Is he someone we're supposed to know?" Trish asked.

"I know who he is,"Jordan said, opening packages of Splenda and emptying them into her coffee. "Loose Cannon is what everybody calls him. His name has been attached to all kinds of disreputable deals, crooked financing, bad mortgages. I don't know how he stays in business, but he does. There must be dozens of people out there who wanted him dead."

"Misti may not even know about his business," Cay said. "She seems sort of innocent, in an odd way. She sure didn't seem to know much about her newly acquired groom."

"Not to change topics, but let's talk about me. I'm going to divorce that sonofabitch I call my husband," Jordan said.

"What?" Trish almost dropped the cup in her hand. "Jordan, maybe I should put something stronger in here than coffee. What 's Jim done this time?"

"What has he done? Exactly nothing. Exactly the same thing he has or hasn't done since we got married."

"Did he say anything about your hair? " Cay asked.

"Oh, about the hair. See it?" Jordan pulled a bright red curl away from her head and let it spring back. "Thirty-nine-ish years I'm a blond, I've known Jimmy for twenty-some of those years, and did he notice? He did not."

"Maybe he didn't say anything because it was a shock," Trish said.

"Maybe he didn't like it and didn't want to say so," Cay said.

"No. If Jimmy doesn't like something, he says, 'The dog peed on my shoes,' or 'The bumper on your car is missing. ' Just straight declarative sentences. No, Jimmy didn't even see my hair. To him I don't exist."

* * *

"I think we have covered the basics," Lanier said. "Remember, Misti, when you speak to the police, answer them honestly, but keep it short. Answer only what they ask and do not elaborate. Understand?"

Misti nodded vigorously.

"Into the lion's den, then. Don't worry, I'll be right there. You're stronger than you think."

"*You're wrong,*" Misti thought. "*I'm stronger than you think.*"

Chapter 4

"This has certainly been a lively start to the day," Cay said. "I was expecting to be bored unwrapping knick-knacks and helping Andrea get unpacked next door. But, here we are in the Women's Justice Center with another murder mystery to solve. Our LitChix Book Club will be so jealous." She settled herself into one of the overstuffed chairs.

"I'm starved," Jordan said, bringing in cheese and crackers from the kitchen. "You have to get more food in this place."

Misti was eating a peanut butter sandwich, curled up with Mr. Chanel on a sofa. "This is such a cozy room," she said looking around.

"That is Andrea's doing," Trish nodded. "Cuz, you definitely have a flair for decorating. You've done a good job on your wonderful house next door, too. Using your furniture from your old home was a great idea."

Andrea said, "I wanted the ladies who are helped here to know they are valuable people. Some will be living here and some will be coming in during the day to use the services we will offer. The oriental rugs, antique furnishings and three-hundred thread count sheets let them know they are appreciated and worthwhile. I got sick of those things at Chateau Soleil. I love seeing them here, being used and enjoyed."

Misti took some cheese and a cracker. "Andrea, I would have thought you would prefer living in Buckhead and just volunteering down here in Grant Park like so many other fancy ladies do."

"No. I like living in Grant Park now." Andrea said. "This building and the house next door were pretty run down when I got them, as you recall, but with a lot of remodeling they are starting to look good. This brick building was an old church with a warren of classrooms and offices. Those were easy to convert into bedrooms for the residents. The commercial kitchen and huge dining room are perfect for our needs. My house next door is authentic Cottage-style, and it has a lot of years on it, but it is solid and it is going to be a beauty. "

Trish asked, "How are Missy and EJ doing? I remember your kids weren't too thrilled to leave Chateau Soleil and the West Paces Ferry life and move to Grant Park."

Jordan brightened, "Maybe the students at the Westminster School bubble could visit the WJC and Grant Park for a field trip. You know, a cultural excursion."

Andrea frowned at Jordan. "Any way, the move was an adjustment, especially for image-conscious teenagers, but they like it now. I'd even say they like it a lot. They feel more urban and cosmopolitan and laugh at how sheltered they were in Buckhead. This neighborhood is working out well for all of us. Besides, it's the perfect location for the abused women we will be serving."

Jordan spread some cheese from a little brown crock on a cracker. "Damn, this stuff is addictive," she said. "Have you had it in the fridge since Christmas? That's the only time I see it. Never mind, back to the topic. Misti, tell us everything."

Misti told Andrea and the Chix the same story she told Lanier, confessing she had only known Lew a few weeks before they eloped to Vegas. "We weren't supposed to date the customers, but you know how that works. He kind of wore me down after a while and we started going out, but in a real low key kind of way."

Warming to her subject, Misti continued. "Plus, I couldn't go anywhere nice because I was so greasy after my act. I always oiled up my arms and legs real good – not enough so I'd go flying off the pole mind you, but enough to bring out my great muscle definition."

"Another career choice shot down," Cay mumbled and ate a second cracker with cheese.

"As you were saying," Jordan prompted, "you were seeing Lew after hours."

"That's right. We got married just last week. A week ago Saturday, to be exact." Misti teared up. "My sweet bunny boy. I can't believe he's gone." Misti dabbed her eyes and took another bite of her sandwich.

"Well, plan on moving into the Justice Center," Andrea said. "Your place is a crime scene, and you wouldn't want to stay there anyway."

"You can say that," Misti replied. "We weren't there for long, but we made a lot of memories."

"Where is your condo located?" Trish asked.

"It's on Marietta Street, not far from Georgia Tech. Only four condos in the whole building. There are only four floors, plus the main floor. It used to be a warehouse, so it's concrete inside and some brick – kinda cold, but Lew and me made it warm."

"Could there have been anyone else in the building who saw anything this morning?" Trish asked.

"I don't think so. We are the only tenants so far."

"How do you think Lew's killer could have gotten in?" Trish asked. "Did anyone else have a key?"

"Gee, that's a good question. Lanier and the cops asked the same thing. I don't know the answer to that one." Misti looked up. "Do any of you hear a car honking?"

"What?" Andrea said. "I didn't hear it. Cay, you're next to the window. Can you look out and see what's going on?"

Pulling a sheer curtain aside, Cay looked on the street in front of the Women's Justice Center. "Looks like a truck. Maybe it's a moving van. Anyway, it seems to be blocking traffic."

"Mother!" Andrea exclaimed. "How could have I forgotten? Mother and Isabelle are moving in today. Quick, someone run out there and direct them around to the parking lot in back. Jordan, you are pretty agile. You go too, Cay, and clear some of those boxes out of the back hall so that they can get in. Trish, you can help her? I'll take Misti upstairs and find her a room."

"I thought that they were already living here," Trish said.

"Yes and no," Andrea answered, "Mother wanted to leave a few things in her house until they sold it – makes it look more inviting. Isabelle is bringing her ridiculous book collection today."

"How can you call a book collection ridiculous?" Cay asked. "I'd call it sacred."

"Well, if you call hundreds of paperbacks with bare chested men and big bosomed women on the covers sacred, then it is about the most sacred collection I've ever seen. Isabelle has kept every romance novel she ever bought, and she bought a ton of them," said Andrea.

Trish frowned. "You know, I would never have guessed Isabelle would love romance novels. She is so practical and efficient. She even dresses in a business-like manner. Obviously she has a secret, more sensitive side to her personality."

Andrea continued, "There are now shelves in the library and that's where the books are going. Isabelle agreed to share them with our future residents."

"I don't know if that's a good idea; I suggested it in a weak moment. We'll have to wait and see. So, anyway, Isabelle and Mother have bedrooms here but they still owned their house. Now, no more house. This is their home."

"Great," Misti said. "I was afraid I'd be here all alone. It will be like a slumber party. I've never had one of those."

"You never had a slumber party, even when you were a little girl?" Andrea asked as they climbed the stairs to the bedrooms.

"No. There was no place for any more kids in our trailer, and anyway..." Her voice trailed off and she was silent.

Andrea let the subject drop. "Well, look around. You pretty much have your pick except for the first two on the right. Those belong to Mother and Isabelle."

Misti tiptoed down the wide, carpeted hallway, as if she were in a sanctuary. She opened each door, peeked inside and then quietly closed it. When she came to the door opposite Isabelle's she said, "This is it. Can I have this one? It has pink curtains, and pink is my favorite color."

"Then it's yours", "Andrea said. "Welcome home". *At least for now.* Andrea thought. *Misti will get back on her feet and move on, but for now it was important that she have a sense of ownership.*

Misti tiptoed into the room, lay down on the bed and was fast asleep in minutes.

A murder is exhausting, Andrea thought, *and I'm a girl who knows. First there is all that adrenaline, and then you just crash. Poor Sonny. It seems ages ago I found him dead with barbeque sauce poured all over him, but it has been only a few months. Life is full of the oddest twists and turns.*

Chapter 5

It wasn't that far from the Women's Justice Center to Misti's condo, but Atlanta traffic was slow. "Honest to God," Detective Helen Morrow said as she turned right to get on a less traveled street. "That group of women gets crazier by the minute."

"What do you mean?" Bongiovanni said pressing his feet against the floor mats as if that would slow down the Crown Vic. "They aren't so bad, compared to some we've seen."

"Are you kidding me? First there's Andrea Simmons who is slumming it, playing Lady Bountiful, and then that cousin of hers, the good widow Trish Townsend, oh so proper, with a pole up her ass, and Cay whatever, with those clodhoppers and little girl socks, and now red-headed Miss New Jersey 1985..."

"Now wait a minute," Bongiovanni laughed. "I thought you were the one who didn't judge. What's with the attitude?"

"They're annoying. First of all, you can't tell me Miss Buckhead Blue Eyes didn't get away with murdering her husband. She batted her eyes and flashed her dough and..."

Jerry interrupted, "You know there was plenty of evidence to exonerate Mrs. Simmons."

Helen slammed on brakes and hit her hand on the steering wheel. "Maybe she didn't pull the trigger, but I would bet money that she was in on it somehow. Maybe sock girl, Cay Curtis, is a dead shot. Trish might be an expert in poison. Jordan wouldn't hesitate to hit a two-timing man hard enough to do some serious damage. Who knows what that bunch is really capable of. The way they stick together is suspicious to me."

"I never thought you were prejudiced, Morrow. Cay is just not into the fashion thing. She's an intellectual who consults with libraries and private collectors for a living. Hard to believe she can make a lot of money doing that though. As for the rest of them, I think you are jealous they found the clues to exonerate Andrea and we didn't."

Helen cursed at a car turning left in front of her, holding up traffic. "That's another thing. If Cay's so smart, what is she doing with the rest of them? Add their I.Q's together and it still wouldn't equal the average pile of rocks. Besides none of them can be very smart if they think that Justice Center is going to succeed."

"Boy, you are pissed off, aren't you? Hey, you're pretty damn cute when you're mad, you know." Bongiovanni knew that remark would make Helen even angrier, and he was right. She snapped on the siren.

"Seriously, Helen, is there something wrong? This isn't like you. Do you need some time off?"

"No. Forget it. I just want to get out of this damn traffic and get to the Cannons' condo already."

"Ah, the Jersey 'already'. I see I'm rubbing off on you." Helen showed no reaction. She pulled past cars and hopped curbs until she was in the clear. In a few minutes she parked in front of the condo building. The Georgia Crime Scene Unit techs were already there, and yellow tape was strung up outside the front door.

"This may be the perfect crime scene. No one lives in this building but the dead guy and his pole dancing wife.

No witnesses." Jerry looked at the blank name plates above three of the four intercoms on the blockish, uninviting building. The name on the fourth one read M. Hozk. "What kinda name is that?"

Helen stared. "You're from Jersey. You tell me. Maybe Eastern European. How in the hell would you pronounce it?" she said, making a mental note to follow up on the name.

Jerry pushed open the front door. He and Helen stepped into the cavernous hallway that ran around three sides of the central core. Gleaming polished concrete floors gave off a cold shine, reflecting light from a narrow skylight fifty feet above. The detectives pulled on latex gloves.

"Cozy," Helen said. "Reminds me of the federal pen. Same warm, bunker-like charm. I guess each condo is sort of a U shape, am I right? Three sides around the elevator core."

"What would you have to sell these babies for to make any money with only four units? If you ask me, it's downright ugly," Bongiovanni said.

"Did you notice when we came in there was no landscaping?" Morrow said. "Just bare ground, some broken concrete. Wonder how old these lofts are. We need to trace the ownership of the building." Helen stepped into the elevator . "Come on, Jerry, let's go for a ride."

The elevator was featureless. The polished stainless steel walls appeared print free, but they would be dusted thoroughly for fingerprints by the crime scene team. The Berber carpet covering the floor would be vacuumed and probed and then removed for more testing. The Georgia Crime Scene Unit never knew where a trace could pop up and tell its story. The elevator opened directly into Misti and Lew's foyer.

"Wow," Jerry said.

"Back at ya," Helen replied. "What did Misti say Lew did for a living? I didn't know low-end realtors made this kinda money."

The foyer was paneled in unfilled cream-colored marble. A tall metal sculpture that looked like one of Giacometti's attenuated women stood to one side of a mirrored Donghia Louis XIV style chest. A Georgia O'Keefe of a cavernous lily, hung against a creamy marble wall, and a tall arch to the left opened to the living room.

A tech called from the bedroom area."Hey, Detectives, come in here." Jerry and Helen hurried through the living room, glancing briefly at the perfectly lit paintings on the walls and a decorator's dream of eclectic perfection. The master bedroom was off a short hall.

"Look in here," a young female tech said, pointing her flashlight beam into the closet.

"Jesus!" Jerry yelped. "Why didn't you warn me. I almost stepped on the son of a bitch."

"At least that confirms what Misti said, about not seeing him until she was walking into her closet," Helen said. "God damn, he is one ugly mother. Is that a toupee beside him? A really bad toupee?"

"Don't speak ill of the dead, Morrow," Jerry said. "And yeah, it is pretty bad. He's tall, too. Must be six foot five or six. He's a whole lot of ugly. I assume this is Lew Cannon. He would certainly attract attention."

Helen laughed in spite of herself.

The tech glanced at her clipboard. "We've photographed everything in this room. We'll be looking for fiber evidence, prints and so forth for the rest of the day, probably more. Look at this – this is what I wanted you to see." The tech spotlighted a shelf about eight feet above the floor on the left of the closet. "See that?" Her light swiveled down to play on several screws on the floor. "Those screws were supposed to support the top shelf. They were pulled out and, look, the front of the shelf fell down. Looks like it made a runway for that bowling ball down there on the floor," and with that she flashed her light next to Lew Cannon's head. "I'd say that bowling ball rolled straight down the shelf and smashed him in the head. Did you see he was wearing a toupee?"

"Thank you for your detecting," Bongiovanni said, his voice showing annoyance at the tech drawing conclusions that were reserved for detectives, in his opinion.

"Jerry, look at the stuff over here." Helen was standing on what was apparently Misti's side of the closet. On the shelf above her clothes was a line of wig stands, each topped with a wig of a different color. "The hot pink is festive, and the yellow 'little Dutch girl' braids are almost scary. Oh, and the clothes aren't much better. Nothing from Talbots in here. Lots of fishnet and fringe, along with a little black leather."

"Yeah, well, I guess pole dancing has its own dress code," Jerry said. "Come out here with me, Morrow," Jerry led the way into the hall. "I don't want to discuss this in front of the tech. A little too eager. What is your take on that?" and he pointed back toward the bedroom.

"It looked fake to me," Morrow said. "Would a bowling ball really have enough momentum to kill somebody just rolling down a shelf? It isn't all that far, and Lew was pretty tall. How would the killer rig it? The screws would have to come out at just the right second, and he would have to be in the perfect spot. My first instinct is always the wife, but how would she get up there? Misti is only a little over five feet tall. I didn't see a ladder or a chair anywhere."

"Yeah, but remember she's strong and pretty athletic," Jerry interjected.

"What, are you saying?" Morrow asked. "That she swung from a clothes rod or something? She's not as stupid as she wants you to believe, at least that's what I think. However if she was going to off him she would have done a better job than this. There are just too many 'what ifs' in this scenario. I believe her ditsy broad thing is an act. At this point though nothing says 'motive' to me yet."

"Jesus, look at this place. This condo and the art, if it's real, must be worth millions. That seems like a pretty good motive to me." Bongiovanni made a few quick notes on the pad he pulled from his coat pocket.

They walked into the master bathroom. "Maybe. One strange thing..."

Bongiovanni interrupted, "Just one?"

"Funny. What I mean is, something you never find at a crime scene. Do you see how clean this place is? I don't mean neat – I mean sterilized. Do you smell bleach? I smell it. Look there isn't a drop of water on the shower floor and I'll make a wild guess there are no finger prints anywhere. Not even Misti or Lew's. It looks like their condo has been prepped to show."

"You mean to show to a buyer? You think someone came in to look at the condo under the pretenses of being a buyer and offed the guy?" Bongiovanni asked.

"No. More like 'staged to show to a cops who come to look at a crime scene,'" Morrow replied.

"Maybe the killer hid while Misti ran out of the apartment and then wiped everything down," Bongiovanni said.

Helen walked back into the master and pointed to the King-sized bed. "This bed looks as if it hasn't been slept on." Morrow turned to one of the techs. "Be sure and check the sheets and the towels. I bet they are squeaky clean. In fact, check everything for any kind of fibers or trace evidence. I have never seen a crime scene this sterilized."

Bongiovanni's cell phone buzzed. He listened a minute, said, "You're shittin' me," and snapped the phone shut.

"Well?" Helen asked.

"You know that ugly sucker in there with his head bashed in? He doesn't exist. No prints on file, no credit cards, no social, nothing. Driver's license is a fake. No Lew Cannon. I think we need to find out who this guy really is before we worry too much about who killed him."

Chapter 6

"Hey, Jordan. You're early. I made arrangements for the owner to meet us here in ten minutes." Trish joined Jordan at the Lobby Bar at Twelve in Atlantic Station to look at a condo on the tenth floor.

"Don't turn around, but I think the hunk at the end of the bar is staring at me," Jordan said, giving her skirt a modest little tug and flipping her red curls.

"Who? Where?" Trish looked around trying to see Jordan's mystery man.

"Oh, that's just great. Now he's probably laughing at us. Sit down and order something." Jordan fixed her attention on the Cosmopolitan in front of her.

"He was probably just being friendly." Trish smiled at the bartender. "I'll have a diet Coke please. Jordan, get real. Every man in here is ten years younger than we are. Do you really want to be a cougar?" Trish took a sip of her drink. "Don't answer that."

"Trish, it is time for you to start dating again," Jordan said raising her glass in a toast. "You have been a widow long enough. I know your friends have tried to introduce you to eligible men. You have to stop saying you aren't ready and just jump in the crick, or whatever you Southerners jump into when you take the plunge again."

She looked Trish up and down. "Lose the pearls and the beige. You're way too conservative."

Trish glanced at Jordan's attire, "Bill Blass works for me. I'll stick to the basics for now. Besides, don't forget, you are still married. If you want to go out and hit the bars, you really should be legally separated, at least."

Trish glanced at the front of the bar area, then looked at her watch again. She redialed the condo owner's cell. "Oh, dear. I keep getting a recording saying Peter Grimm has a full mailbox. Some realtor, if he doesn't keep up with his messages. He is over an hour late."

Jordan put down her glass. "Peter Grimm? His name is Peter Grimm? What a horrible name."

Trish stood. "Maybe we should view the condo without him. This is too rude."

Jordan waved to the man at the end of the bar. "Good thing for me you still have your real estate license. Can you get us in without him? If you can, let's go."

Making their way through the crowd toward the residential side of Twelve, the two could not have been a greater contrast. With her carefully highlighted blond hair and camel-colored Dana Buchman suit, Trish epitomized good taste. Her leopard print Chanel shoes were the only adventurous aspect of her wardrobe.

Thanks to her flaming red tresses, tight Diesel jeans, and red snakeskin cowboy boots, Jordan's appearance screamed 'Look at me.' Jordan smiled brightly at a good-looking guy. "Do you think I should get cards made up to hand out to hot guys? 'Need a date? Call Jordan, 404 I M ready'."

"Jordan that is the tackiest thing I've ever heard!" Trish started walking faster. "Solicitation. Surely things like that would shock your Jersey friends, too."

"Oh, no. They'd be proud. They'd even get me a deal on the printing." Seeing the look on Trish's face,

Jordan laughed. "I'm kidding, Trish. For God's sake, don't lose your sense of humor."

"Jordan, one of the reasons I love you is that you are crazy. Just don't take your own ideas too seriously. Then I'll begin to worry." Trish pressed the elevator door and when it opened, she ushered Jordan inside.

Chapter 7

Entering the vacant condo, Jordan gasped, "I love it! Look at that view! Hardwood floors, granite countertops! Don't know what it costs, but I want it."

"I am so glad we came without Mr. Grimm. Jordan, you never gush like that in front of a seller. You have to give yourself some negotiating room." Trish studied the informational brochure again. "OK, he is asking four hundred twenty five thousand for two bedrooms, two baths. But, this is only the first property you've seen. Don't you think you should see at least one more before you make an offer?"

"Trish, I love this place! The view of the downtown skyline is breath-taking; the world is at my feet here: the shops, the restaurants, the shops, the banks, the shops all within walking distance. Look! There's the Arts Center." Jordan stepped out onto the balcony. "Oh, look! Lean to the left and you can see the midtown high rises from here. What more could I want?" Jordan did a little boogie dance. "I can order room service from the hotel 24 hours a day. Hot damn; this is cheaper than a round the world cruise! I could stay here forever. If Michael goes to Georgia Tech in the fall, he could practically bicycle there. This is a killer condo! I love it. Twelve. That has such a sophisticated ring. I live at Twelve. Pick me up at Twelve."

"Wait a minute. You want a bachelor pad for yourself and you plan to live in it with your eighteen year-old son? Think about that for a minute, Jordan. That really is crazy. You need to get a grip on what you really want before you start putting half a mil into real estate." Trish sighed and pulled a miniature Milky Way from her purse. "I'll call Peter's office later to make a low ball offer. Jordan, you better let me do the negotiations. You're practically salivating, and that is not the signal you want to send out to get a good deal. Will you consider my suggestion of a lease-purchase? At least until you and Jim go to counseling."

"I'm doing my counseling with Dr. Jack Daniels, thank you. But, as long as I have first option to buy, a lease-purchase would make more sense until my alimony is finalized." Jordan made a face. "What a yucky name for a realtor, Peter Grimm. Mrs. Grimm and all the little Grimms must be a cheery bunch at neighborhood parties."

Trish grinned. "While I agree Grimm Real Estate is a terrible name, it does suit his primary business which specializes in reclaiming toxic properties. I'll keep trying to touch base with Mr. Grimm."

"That's hilarious. 'Hello, Ma'am. I have a beautiful little place for sale on Love Canal.' Don't you lose this condo for me, Trish. This is my new image personified: sophisticated, urban, worldly. My brain is in high gear, placing my furniture in this room already. It's going to be the new me! I can see sage green walls. Silk plaid draperies with sage green, taupe, and brown. My African prints over the sofa. Call Peter's cell again from the car. Make a lowball offer. I know, play it cagey. But Trish, I love it so much."

"Are you sure this is what you want? One day you are dissatisfied with Jim and now you are thinking about buying a condo with alimony you don't have. What do you really want, Jordan?"

"To tell you the truth, Trish, I don't know myself. Sometimes I feel I am literally spinning."

"All the more reason, then, to take it slowly. Don't make any huge commitments. Jordan, there are lots of people who love you and want only the best for you. The Chix especially are here to support you and talk any time night or day. Sometimes talking to a caring person helps a lot."

"I can think of lots of things to do besides talking to a caring person right now," Jordan said. "Seeing Bongiovanni again sure didn't help in that department. He is not the smoothest guy in the world, or the best looking, but he has something that just stops me dead in my tracks. It isn't just the Jersey accent. Oh, that helps, all right, but it's a lot more than that."

"Then maybe you should stay away from him while you are making up your mind about your marriage,"

"Funny, I was thinking just the opposite," Jordan said.

Chapter 8

Pulling out of Twelve, and negotiating the Atlanta traffic, Jordan hurled her car into the right turn lane. She waved out the window and smiled charmingly, counting on someone to let her cut in. As soon as someone motioned to her to come over, she headed back in the direction of the Women's Justice Center.

"I'm having no luck getting Grimm." Trish closed her cell phone, barely suppressing a laugh. "Sorry, I can't help it. He does have such an awful name."

"It is pretty sad, isn't it?" Jordan said. "Grim, even."

That refueled Trish's laughter. "Where are we going? I thought we were heading back to Buckhead."

"I'd rather go back to the Justice Center," Jordan said. "See if Andrea needs help. I should go home sometime, but I dread it. Any place is better right now."

"It isn't the same for me at home either since John's death. Even before then, his grown daughters had moved out and it seemed so quiet. Trey is a typical seventeen year old who is with his friends all the time. He misses his Dad." Trish sighed. "Besides, Andrea is like a drama-magnet. Excitement follows in her wake and home seems so dull by comparison. I know women in trouble like Misti are the motivation for Andrea to create the Justice Center. But dang, Misti could be in serious trouble unless the police can find some reason someone else wanted to kill her husband. I believe her story, but I'm wondering if the police will."

Jordan laid on her horn to encourage the Ford Escort ahead of her to move faster. "I cannot stand it when people don't gun it when the light changes. Speaking of believable scenarios, I know Andrea is committed to helping Misti, but are we sure she's innocent? After all, she could have married for Lew for money and then made his death look accidental. Andrea is using some of Sonny's ill-gotten millions to help 'women in peril,' but what do we really know about Misti besides what she has told us?"

"Gosh. I guess we don't know much about her". Trish said. "Misti was trying to get out of an abusive relationship, and Andrea let her live her briefly while the place was being remodeled. We never met the accused man, but she seemed to want to improve her life. She only stayed in the WJC about three days, and then moved out with a girl friend. While she was there, she seemed eager to get a fresh start. Even talked about enrolling in Vet Tech School." Trish jerked her head toward the car next to Jordan's. "Did that man just give you the finger?"

"Hell, that's Jersey's state bird. Ignore him." Jordan smiled and waved. "All I know is, Misti had opportunity, and her alibi of being in the shower is unverified, and even a little suspicious." She pulled into the HOV lane ignoring the horn blaring behind her. "Wonder if Lew had a will and or insurance, and if so, who is the beneficiary. It's important to know things like that. It would provide her with a strong motive for murder. I don't think we should rush into defending her without investigating further."

"Nobody asked the LitChix to defend her, Jordan. The WJC is paying Lanier to do that." Trish tightened her grip on the dashboard.

"I know, but if it weren't for us and our sleuthing, Andrea might still be dressed in that horrid orange jumpsuit. We do love to play amateur detectives, and damn, we're good."

Trish frowned. "Cay complained about how much time she spent away from her job when we were sleuthing to clear Andrea. She might not be willing to help Misti."

"Yeah, well, I have my own issues. I need to work out with a personal trainer. I caught my reflection in the frozen food section and there was a huge ass following me. Besides Cay loves a mystery as much as we do, and we keep running into women who need rescuing. I'm sure Cay likes helping others whenever she can. She may play up that practical Mid-Westerner thing, but she is a sucker for a hard-luck story, and Misti makes a good case for being needy."

As she negotiated her van toward the Justice Center, Jordan realized something she would never admit to anyone. She actually enjoyed living in Atlanta now. Her complaints were habitual and friends expected her to compare everything unfavorably to her beloved Jersey. It was the friendship with Trish and Cay that started the change.

Jordan's thoughts returned to her situation. She knew her marriage was at a critical stage, but she loved running into Detective Jerry Bongiovanni. After all, he was Italian, from Jersey, and reminded her of a tall, young Stanley Tucci with his dark, brooding good looks. She needed to feel young and interesting, and Jerry just might take the bait.

She thought *"I'll think about that tomorrow. Dear God, I'm starting to sound like Scarlet O'Hara. Shit, I need a trip to Jersey soon."* She blew her horn as she passed the car ahead on the right.

Chapter 9

"Hey Cay? Wha'sup?" Jordan shifted the phone to her other ear.

"This minute? I have a terrible rash and I'm eating frosting out of the can."

"Bad day, huh?"

"No, not especially. Why?"

"Andrea asked Trish to take Misti shopping. She is driving Andrea crazy, going through everything in her closet. All of Misti's stuff is still at the crime scene, so when she says she has nothing to wear, she means it. Misti needs some decent clothes to wear. There is just something about her preference for fishnet stockings and crotchless panties that undermines her credibility as a responsible, and this is important, innocent, wife, if you know what I mean. Anyway, Trish was going to take her to Lenox Square, but Misti says she doesn't want to go there. Says she doesn't shop retail." Jordan sighed. "She wants to go to some places on Buford Highway, flea markets and bargainadas if you can imagine. I'm game. Shopping is my favorite sport."

Cay could hear Misti in the background saying something about "up-tight Buckhead old lady clothes."

"I think I understand."

Jordan said, "All I know about Buford Highway is the Havana Sandwich Shop. Fantastic Cuban Sandwiches. So if Trish has to go, we ought to go too and combine the ridiculous with the sublime. Want us to pick you up?"

"No. I'll meet you all there. I have to walk my dog and give her some attention. I spend so much time with you guys I need to hire a dog walker. Anyway, although shopping isn't my thing, but if there is food involved, I'm game. If you get there first, order me a Cuban. That, and some flan, could cure anything, and it's more nutritious than a can of frosting."

* * *

The Chix and Misti miraculously got a table at the height of the lunch rush. Actually, it wasn't a miracle, it was Misti. Men stared at her form fitting satiny blue top paired with black Valentino pants and her wrap-around shades, courtesy of Andrea. Andrea nearly wept to see her Chanel sunglasses go out the door on Misti, who turned nearly every head in the Sandwich Shop. Men couldn't do enough for her. Misti compounded the effect by simply taking it as her due and letting them grovel, seeming to ignore all of them. Jordan tossed her red curls and got some appreciative glances, but Misti was obviously the plat du jour, as they say in the restaurant biz. She stayed at their table while the Chix went to the counter to place their orders.

"I'll have one of those Cuban sandwiches," Trish said, "and a club soda. With lime, please."

"You can't be serious," Jordan said. "She'll have a Malta and a Cuban. We'll all have that," she said to the woman behind the counter, completely confusing Trish who had no idea what was being ordered. They picked up four iced Maltas and joined Misti while waiting for their order numbers to be called.

"I need a glass." Trish said looking around for a waiter.

"No you don't. Trish, sometimes you have absolutely no sophistication." Jordan took a long pull from the bottle, sighed happily, and looked around the room. "That's why I love this place."

"The food?" Cay asked.

"No. The parking lot. Pickups and Porsches. And they are all in here. Brokers and yard guys and doctors and glamour boys – what a selection! Last time I was here I saw the Atlanta Chief of Police with his bodyguards and the weatherman from Channel 3 all packed into this little shed with the yard guys from the Brookhaven condos and finacial center types."

"Jordan, we have to focus on shopping," said Cay.

"I am shopping. You shop your way and I'll shop mine. Misti, you're directing this. Where do we go after we eat?"

Misti had been quiet, but she began to show more enthusiasm as she talked about clothes. She didn't know the names of most of the shops. She identified them by their proximity to a Dollar Store, a CVS, or a restaurant. She seemed to know exactly where she wanted to go.

"We'll finish at one of the knock-off places," Jordan said. "I want a Louis Vuitton carry-on."

"Jordan, those are so expensive." Trish had never known Jordan to spend a lot on status items.

"I know. It'll be at least thirty dollars. Maybe more."

"Thirty dollars? Are you joking?"

"She's talking about fakes," Cay said.

"Oh. Is that legal?"

Jordan rolled her eyes. "Remind me again why I love you, Trish."

Chapter 10

"Are you finding what you want?" Trish called to Misti. She was on the far side of a long table outside a low building heavily fortified with burglar bars.

"Yeah, I got some stuff. But I still need jeans." She was rifling through a pile of denim cut-offs when she leaned forward and Andrea's Chanel sunglasses dropped onto the asphalt.

"Oh Jesus, Mary and Joseph. Andrea will shit a brick." She bent down to pick them up just as something whizzed over her head.

"What was that?" Trish asked. "Did you just hear a funny noise? Like something hitting metal."

"There's plenty of that," Cay said, looking at the corrugated metal that made up the front of the store.

"Nothing more out here," Misti said. "I'm going inside."

The Chix heard a scream from inside the store. Trish was the first to reach Misti, standing near the cash register, pointing in horror and shrieking at the top of her lungs. There in front of her, a small man was slumped on the floor, a red stain spreading down the front of his shirt.

"Omigosh," Trish said. "Call an ambulance. 911. Somebody, help!" Misti had been corralled by Jordan, who had taken her to the far side of the store. Cay looked dazed.

"All right, I'll call. Cay, you get a towel or something and see if you can stop the blood." Trish's hands shook as she took her cell phone out of her purse.

"I called 911." A girl, who looked very young, was already on the phone. An older woman rushed from a back room and knelt beside the bleeding man. She pulled open his shirt and pressed a towel to his shoulder.

"Whaaa happened?" Cay finally was able to speak.

The woman answered, "Shot. Shoulder. Not look too bad."

"Any gunshot is bad," Cay said.

"Who? How? There is no one here with a gun, and nobody ran out the front door," Trish's voice now shaking as much as her hands.

"Out there. Drive-by." The woman pointed toward the street.

Just then the paramedics and the police came, and the news media in their satellite trucks pulled up and started taking pictures and asking for interviews. It seemed all too familiar.

Chapter 11

Bongiovanni hadn't blown coffee out his nose since the morning years before when his teenage son announced he was quitting school and going on the road with his thirty-year old musician girlfriend. A lack of talent and cash brought them back soon enough, but it was a feeling you don't forget.

Here was the feeling once again when he turned on the six o'clock news and saw the video. The photographer was shooting low to capture the scene of the shopkeeper slumped on the tile floor. He captured a little more than that: in the foreground were a pair of women's Birks, worn with Hello Kitty pink and black socks. They almost certainly belonged to Cay Curtis. As the camera panned upward, a woman's wild eyes above a brown paper bag over her nose and mouth confirmed her identity. No doubt about it. It was Cay, and if Cay were at the scene of a crime, the rest of the Chix must be there, too. *It's just the odds*, Bongiovanni thought.

The camera held fast, catching Misti's cleavage as she bent over to give Cay a pat on the back. The crawl read, "Drive-by shooting wounds DeKalb store owner." At least nobody got killed this time. DeKalb. *That's good. Not my jurisdiction anyway*, he thought. *Maybe I'll give Red a call, get some more details, say some reassuring words, that kind of stuff. Wonder if she is still thinking about that eggplant parm. Naw, that's not necessary. Hell, I'm just being professional, that's all.*

There was that itchy feeling at the back of his throat, the one that always signaled something wasn't quite right. He used to put it off to an allergy or a cold coming on, but as he got older, he knew those weren't the causes. It was unease about something in his life. Evidence that bothered him, sometimes a woman who bothered him. This time it was women, plural.

There was Misti Cannon, the prime suspect in her husband's murder, no real alibi, but no hard evidence against her either. Research showed the condo was in her name and paid for with cash. Although it hadn't been verified, he'd bet his badge the paintings and all the expensive furnishings were in her name, too. Did Lew give them to her or did pole dancing pay more than he thought? She sure as hell didn't tell the whole story when he and Morrow interviewed her that first morning, all bundled up and supposedly scared. Who was Lew Cannon, anyway? That mess wasn't sorted out yet. And Jordan - Red. Not free, not a good idea, but she was in his mind all the time, like a song that gets stuck in your head and won't go away.

Now this drive-by nagged him. Years on the force told him there was a connection to Lew, that it was not a coincidence the Chix were in the same area. He was beginning to think someone wanted Misti dead too. Just a hunch, no evidence. But you can take a cop's hunch to the bank especially if he's lost most of his hair and good deal of his shoe leather just being a cop – a good, thorough cop.

Chapter 12

"I'm fixing' to get my ass arrested." Misti pulled on the hem of her skirt as she seated herself at Brio with Lanier and the Chix.

"They'll probably take the rest of you, too." Cay said. "Men do seem to think your tush is a lethal weapon."

"Looks like the police believe I killed my beloved Lew. OK, so we only knew each other a month or so. OK, so we'd only been married ten days. OK, it was my bowling ball that whacked my poor Bunny-Boy, but why would the police think I killed my husband? Was there a shred of evidence? There was not, because I didn't do it."

"Welcome to Bigo, I mean Brio," stammered the stunned waiter, before reciting the list of the day's specials.

Lanier restrained himself from ordering for everyone and let the Chix and Misti tell the waiter their own choices. When the waiter moved away from their table, Lanier began to explain the court procedure to Misti in the event she was arrested.

"You will be brought before the judge and charged with murder. Of course, you will plead 'not guilty.' I'll be right there with you." Lanier patted Misti's hand. "The Women's Justice Center will put up your bail, if the judge will grant it, and maybe we can get you released under their supervision."

Trish leaned toward Misti, "Misti, you do understand if you run away, you could jeopardize the financial stability not to mention the creditability of the Justice Center."

"Yeah, yeah, yeah. Andrea's a little tight-ass, but I'd never screw her."

Overhearing the conversation as he approached their table, the waiter's hands shook so much the lobster bisque sloshed over the sides of the bowl and some splashed onto Mitsi's bare leg. She squealed, jumped up, and dashed to the ladies' room.

"Omigosh! Omigosh! I hope she's OK. I am so sorry." The waiter looked as if he were going to cry.

"Don't worry," Jordan said. "She's had hotter things than lobster bisque on her thigh."

Cay rolled her eyes. "Lanier, as you were saying."

"You Chix are cheaper by the hour than I am. Ya'll need to brainstorm with Misti to try to discover who wanted Lew Cannon dead. So far she is the only suspect."

"It'll be the first time Misti's brain was stormed. She is one crayon short of a box."

"Hush, Jordan, she's coming back," Cay gave Jordan a nudge.

"She must be coming back because there is a breeze from every man turning in her direction." Jordan brightened. "I just love the idea of sleuthing. How lucky we are to keep running into women accused of murdering their husbands."

"It's all about keeping you happy, Jordan," said Cay.

Lanier took control of the conversation. "OK Misti, to get things started, let's go over the facts again to see if there is something else you can remember. Anything. Start with how you and Lew got together."

Misti went over their unorthodox courtship and their impulsive flight to Vegas to get married.

"How do you pull off a wedding without months of planning?" Trish asked.

"Vegas was created for that! Kelly Ripa did it, so I figured I could, too. I had just enough time to go to the Love Me Tender Chapel powder room to freshen up before saying 'I do'. Oh, wait. There was something odd, well, kinda odd, that happened in there." Misti took a sip of her sweet tea. "A really big lady in a blue sequined dress was in the powder room. She asked if she could borrow my makeup kit. I told her sure, but when I got outta the stall, she was gone and the make-up kit was on the counter. What was odd is I think that lady was a man. You don't see hair on too many women's knuckles. But I figured, what the hell, it's Vegas."

"Are you sure he/she/it didn't steal anything?" Trish asked.

"Hmm, didn't think about that. I was so excited about gettin' married. My purse and my make-up bag are still in our condo. As soon as I can, I'll check and find out." Misti frowned. "But, for now, I can't go back there. The police still have yellow crime scene tape everywhere. The detectives told me so, and that they will tell me when it's clear."

"Field Trip," said Jordan.

Trish turned to Lanier. "Don't the police have any other suspects in Lew's death? Is Misti their only lead? What do they think is her motive for killing him? Lew told her he put the condo in her name, but as far as she knows, he left her no other assets, so money isn't the motive. What is?"

"That's one thing I am counting on the Chix finding out. The police can't find a motive for murder. Right now, they are having a hard time finding clues to Lew's identity so, no, there are no other suspects right now. They are centering on Misti, period." Lanier glanced around the table and smiled. "That's where you all come in. Start sleuthing for leads to the real killer. You proved your detective skills when you uncovered key evidence freeing Andrea. I know you can do the same for Misti. You all are naturals. Maybe reading all those mysteries in your book club has sharpened your instincts for investigating crimes. Just don't do anything illegal or get yourselves in trouble.

"I can tell you that at this point there are no fingerprints or trace evidence which would indicate a third party. The GSU said they never investigated such a sterile home."

"Oh, It's easy to explain," Misti said, pulling her blouse back up on her shoulder. "Lew was such a neat freak. I don't know how he could stand to live with me, because I am pretty messy. He kept everything spotless, and I do mean spotless. You should have seen him running around with his little linen rag and spray bottle. He even wiped the door knobs."

Lanier made a note to himself on his ever-present monogrammed pad of paper. "There is a DNA swab they are testing," Lanier said, "but it can take awhile, unlike on TV. The preliminary report made note of something on his face and maybe in his ear."

"Sorry to leave you all, but I have another appointment at my office. Call me when you have anything to report. Nothing you find is insignificant." Lanier paid the bill and left, while the girls lingered over coffee and desert.

"I really like Brio," Jordan said, looking around the restaurant. "Nice soothing colors, nice soothing waiters." She gave a wink to the young man pouring water into Cary's glass and tugged on her skirt. "I wish that the damn drycleaner would stop shrinking my clothes."

"Maybe," Cay said, "if you would buy a slightly larger size, you wouldn't have the problem with your skirts riding up to your navel."

"Are you suggesting I'm fat?" Jordan asked. "I am exactly the same size I was when I graduated from high school."

"Whatever you say dear," Cay said. "You aren't fat. And you aren't eighteen."

"Speaking of being eighteen with hormones raging, you 've been acting strangely lately, Cay. Wha'sup?"

"I think it's a man," Misti said.

"A man? Are you sure? Do you know? Did she tell you?" Jordan couldn't ask questions fast enough.

"No, she didn't tell me anything. You just know, ya know?"

"Hello. Stop talking about me as if I wasn't right here," Cay said.

"Well, Cay, you certainly have been spending a lot of time at the Monastery of the Holy Spirit in Conyers," Trish said.

Cay retorted. "Unlike some of the people at this table, my life doesn't center on men. I have a paying job and some of us have to work. Besides it's right up my alley."

"What alley?" Jordan asked. "The one filled with unavailable men?"

Cay glared at her. "No, I meant medieval literature. You know what I mean. The monks have quite a trove of beautiful and important illuminated documents. I'm cataloguing them and helping the Brothers figure out what the collection is worth."

"If you're in love with a monk and didn't tell me, I will be so mad," Jordan said.

Cay folded her napkin slowly and deliberately. "If you must know what else I have been doing, I'll tell you, but you are not allowed to make fun of me." Trish and Jordan nodded, so she continued, "Some friends of mine asked me to officiate at their wedding. I couldn't because I didn't have a license, but their request started me thinking.

You know how I love to research, so I went online and found a non-denominational ministry where I could get a license and the materials I would need to legally marry someone, so I did it. I have worked hard to compose a liturgy that uses philosophy, which was my minor in undergrad, and some poetry. Since then, I have done a couple of commitment ceremonies and one wedding. Now you know where I have been spending some of my time away from you all."

"Are these gay weddings legal in Georgia?" Trish asked.

"Commitment ceremonies don't have the force of law, but they aren't illegal and can be very important to the people involved. I've loved performing them."

"So now you are what – Reverend Cay Curtis? Now I know you are really and truly friggin' crazy." Jordan shook her head.

"Well, personally, I think it's great, Cay. Especially if this gives you pleasure and benefits others," Trish said. "At least I think I think so."

"Let's just stick with the idea that this makes me happy. I am helping some people and certainly not hurting anyone."

"You're right, Cay and thanks for explaining. Jordan and I were getting a little concerned about your disappearances.

"Right now Chix, we have more pressing problems," Trish said. "Let's get back to the Center. Mother and Isabelle have taken on the Grand Opening party planning with more enthusiasm than skill, I'm afraid, and Andrea needs us to be there to lend a steadying hand."

"That's the day," Cay said, "when our hands are the steadying ones. Oh, we have come such a long way."

Misti sighed. "So nice of Lanier to take us to lunch. Guys are nicer in your world than mine."

"There are no free lunches in Buckhead either. Lanier will charge Andrea and she'll pay one way or another," said Cay, as they passed the hostess stand heading for the exit.

"Ohhh, I love these mints," Jordan grabbed a handful and dropped them in her bag while she searched for the valet parking ticket.

Embarrassed, Cay reassured the hostess, "She got them for all of us."

Waiting for Jordan's van, the Chix and Misti continued discussing what they would do next to prove her innocence.

"Holy shit. The valet is stealing my van!"

"I've been in your van Jordan. Believe me, he's not stealing it," Cay said.

The van screeched out of the parking lot and shot across Peachtree Street, miraculously missing the steady flow of traffic. It plowed into a defunct gas station before stopping halfway into the plate glass window. The Chix and Misti stood and gaped.

"If the valet is dead, do I still have to tip him?" Jordan asked.

Chapter 13

"Jordan, I don't think I have ever seen you up this early," Isabelle said. "You poor dear. I heard you had a near tragedy yesterday with your car. Pull up a chair and have some breakfast." Isabelle and Mother were in the Justice Center kitchen serving spinach frittatas to Cay, Trish, Andrea and Misti at the kitchen table.

"Orange juice?" Andrea asked, filling the glass in front of Jordan before she answered.

"Coffee," Jordan was able to finally get the word out, although it sounded more like "cawfee" with her Jersey accent.

"Know anything more about the accident yesterday?" Andrea asked.

"Good news. Bad news. Good news first: the valet isn't seriously injured. Bad news: my van is out of commission for repairs. The guy at the garage said he'll call me as soon as they checked it out. I know it was no accident." Jordan added six Splendas and filled the coffee cup half-full of cream. "Cay, good to see you," she said. "I've been thinking. It has to be more than a few old books and some weddings occupying your time. Tell me the truth. Are you in love with a monk? I just have this feeling."

"What? Jordan, honestly, where did you get that idea? Let go of it, please. It is such nonsense." Cay sputtered almost spilling her coffee.

"Well, you have been so secretive and we don't see you as much, and well, what else could it be?"

"Actually, I can think of quite a few things I could be doing," Cay said. "But instead of my love life, or its absence, maybe we should talk about these two recent murder attempts. It has to be more than being in the wrong place at the wrong time."

Jordan took a sip of her coffee. "I hate it when people keep trying to kill me."

"I'll say," Misti said. "What's up with that?"

"Maybe you should tell us," Trish said. "This has to be about you, Misti, don't you think?"

"How the hell should I know? I haven't done anything. How do we know Jordan didn't flirt with some guy and his wife is pissed?" Misti folded her hands in her lap in an attempt to look virtuous.

"Me?" Jordan thought a minute and shrugged. "Well, possibly…"

"Jordan, you did tell the police about yesterday's incident, didn't you?" asked Cay.

"Yeah, yeah, yeah. I'll call Bongiovanni after I talk to the garage guy when he finds out what caused the brakes to fail like that. I'm driving a rental for now. It's out back."

"Good, Jordan," Andrea said. "If someone is after you, and I am almost certain no one is, at least they won't recognize your rental. Well, finish breakfast. I have someone for you all to meet. The intercom to the garage apartment is working. I'll ask him to come over."

Trish waited for Misti to take her plate to the kitchen sink and then whispered to Cay and Jordan, "We have to get into the Cannon's condo and sleuth. Maybe we can find something the police missed."

The back door opened and an ebony god right out of a Calvin Klein underwear ad entered the kitchen.

"Everyone," Andrea said, "This is Jackson Randall and that's his dog, Ace. Jackson, you've met Misti, Mother and Isabelle. Now meet my three dear friends, Trish, Cay and Jordan. They call themselves the LitChix, but I'll explain that another time. Jordan, put your eyes back in your head."

"Hello good lookin'," Jordan stood, trying for a May West imitation. "And what do you do, if I may ask, Mr. Randall?" Her breathy voice indicated a persona switch to Marilyn Monroe.

"Well, Ma'am, a little bit of everything, I guess, and please call me Jackson."

"I was hoping you'd say that. Please call me Jordan," She gazed up at his eyes, nearly a foot above hers. "My, what big biceps you have," she said.

"Jordan, you are embarrassing Jackson," Trish said. "Please go on, Jackson. What is it you do here?" Trish was determined to make up for Jordan's leering approach.

"First and foremost, Ma'am, Ace and I are here to protect the residents of the Justice Center." Ace's ears went forward attentively. He looked ready to protect anyone posing a threat. "Besides that, I'm pretty handy at maintenance, and I even cook a little, if I have to."

"Oh, my," Cay said, in spite of herself.

"We could all use some protection, that's for sure," Misti said. "It's been crazy. I don't know what terrible thing will happen next. We seem to attract trouble."

Andrea said, "I told Jackson a little bit about what's been going on. I think that we will all be a lot more comfortable having him live in the apartment above the garage to keep an eye on things."

"I feel so much safer already, I may not even go home," Jordan said. "Jackson, you certainly look fit. What did you do before you came to our Justice Center?"

"I was in the army, Ma'am. I'm a Ranger. I took some shrapnel in the knee in Afghanistan, so that's why I'm here and not still jumping out of choppers. Got a little limp but that doesn't slow me down much. Just like Ace, here. He's got a limp too, but he can still do the job. He worked with a cop friend of mine. Ace was a top drug dog. Too good, I guess, because a dealer tried to take him down. Didn't stop old Ace. He had a bullet in his hip but he had to be pulled off the guy."

"He's a German Shepherd, right?" Trish asked, tentatively patting Ace's head.

"That's right Ma'am. Ace likes to work. He seemed like a natural for this security job. We're a good team. The only thing I have ever seen him back down from is that," and he pointed to Mr. Chanel, sitting on his leopard print dog pillow, a faint snarl curling his upper lip. "That little ol' ball of fluff backed him into a corner first time they met."

"Mr. Chanel is territorial, but he'll get used to Ace being here. Well, since we are all here, I think we need to get to work," Andrea said. "There is some old broken furniture out by the garage that needs to go to the dump."

"No problem, Ma'am. I can take it down there for you," Jackson said.

"Not so fast," Jordan said. " I have a loaner for a few days while my van is in the shop. I got the biggest, baddest truck you ever saw: candy apple red, chrome pipes, deluxe leather interior. You name it, this baby's got it. We can all take it for a spin and drop off the furniture at the dump. I love to drive it." Jordan hopped up and down a couple of times like a kid with a new toy.

"I wondered who that … that truck belonged to," Jackson said. "I would never have guessed it was you, Ma'am."

"And I thought a rental car would make Jordan less noticeable." Andrea said. "Silly me. Well, I'm staying here.

Trish and I need to work on plans for the Open House. Mother and Isabelle can help us, too. We'll be fine."

"Ace can guard y'all," Jackson said.

"Some guard dog. Ace is a cripple!" Misti blurted out. "Sorry, but he's limping and he's even scared of that little white hair ball over there. Maybe I should stay too,"

"Nope. Go with us, Misti," Cay said. "Somebody else has to go in this monster truck and sit in the back with me."

"Well, maybe going with you all will be good for me," Misti said. "I need to get out more."

"There's nothing like a trip to the dump to put a fresh face on things," Cay said.

"That is so true," Misti replied, checking her make-up in the shiny surface of a highly polished sterling creamer on the counter.

After Jackson threw pieces of furniture into the truck bed, Jordan climbed into the driver's seat and sat on two Atlanta phone books so she could see over the dashboard. She patted the seat next to her. "Jackson, you sit up here with me. Misti, you and Cay can have the backseat. This is perfect."

"Perfection is in the eye of the beholder," Cay said.

"You got something in your eye?" Misti asked. "You need a tissue?" She pulled a couple of powder blue tissues out of her bra.

"Oh, no thanks. I'm fine," Cay said. "How did you all get into this vehicle.? I think I need a crane."

"Here, I'll give you a hand, "Misti said, jumping up onto the running board and leaping into the cab. She extended her hand to grasp Cay's. With one swift pull, Cay was on the running board and then into the seat. "See, nothing to it," Misti said. "It's just leverage, plus I am pretty strong. Comes in handy."

"I can see that it does," Cay gasped. "I'm impressed."

"Ready to go? Seatbelts on?" Jordan scanned the passengers as she had done in her car pool days. The truck started with a roar and then idled to a loud purr. "OK, which way to the dump?"

"Your truck has a GPS system," Cay said. "Jordan, just punch in your destination."

"Here, I'll do it," Jackson said.

"Ooh, thank you," Jordan said. "I love a man who takes charge." She jammed the stick shift into gear and pulled into the street without looking for oncoming traffic. "Get outta my way, boys," Jordan shouted. "Mine is bigger than yours!"

Cay closed her eyes.

"Are you tired?" Misti asked.

"I've been trying to pray more lately," Cay said. "This seems like a good time to start."

Chapter 14

"Thank goodness they're gone," Andrea said.

"I've already mixed the cake batter," Mother said. "As soon as I pour it in the pans, I'll come into the dining room and help you decorate."

Trish and Andrea pulled a large box out of the pantry. They carried it into the dining room and put it on the buffet. Isabelle opened it with a box cutter revealing pink, white and green tissue paper streamers, pastel paper plates and cups, birthday banners and other party items suitable for a six year old.

"Do you think the Care Bears theme is a little youthful for Misti?" Trish asked.

"I like it," Andrea said. "True, these are from a birthday party for one of my kids quite a few years ago and we never used them. They are still in their original wrappings."

"You could probably get real money for them on eBay," Trish said, "but go for it. Care Bears party it is."

"It broke my heart when Misti said she had never had a sleep over. Now she'll have a birthday party with a homemade cake and a sleep over. She needs to know people care for her so she can let down her defenses. Besides, every girl is a little girl when it's her birthday."

"How old is she, anyway?" Trish asked.

"That's for Misti to say, if she wants to." Andrea said. "There is no way to guess her age."

"You've got me to keep you honest, Cuz," Trish said. "We are the same age, after all, so we both have to lie, or neither of us."

"I think the forties are a woman's best years," Andrea said. "At least they are for me, so far. I'll let you know if I start to lie about my age so you can, too. But right now I am happier with myself than I have ever been, even if a few lines have started to creep in."

"You have nothing to worry about," Trish said. "Women ten years younger than you wish they looked so good."

"You're sweet," Andrea said. "Enough about me. Let's get to work on Misti's party." Andrea started hanging the streamers in swags from the chandelier. "This is going to be such fun," she said.

Chapter 15

"So, who pimped your ride?"

"Misti, sit back dear. Put your seatbelt back on," Cay said. "Jordan, I think Misti is speaking to you."

"What? Sorry. Driving this thing takes all my attention. What did you say?"

"I said, 'Who pimped your ride?'" Misti repeated. "I never saw a truck like this on your side of town."

"Let's see. I think that was a compliment," Cay said.

Jordan adjusted the rear view mirror. "I don't know who did anything. I got it this way from my dealer while they are working on my van."

"You have a dealer? No shit? Yeah, it looks like a dealer's ride."

"Not that kind of dealer, Misti," Cay said. "Jordan means an automobile dealer."

"Oh, well. anyway, it is really one tricked out truck. Pick up many guys with this? It is a pick-em-up truck, right? I crack myself up." Misti wriggled back and put on her seat belt which made her short skirt ride up higher.

Cay thought, *Lord, please let her be wearing underwear.*

"Anyone want some Juicy Fruit?" Misti offered.

"I do," Jordan replied. "Gum helps me stay on my diet."

"A skinny little thing like you? Men like some meat on their women. Am I right?" She thumped Jackson on the shoulder. He said nothing.

"Are we almost there?" Cay asked, a plaintive note in her voice.

"Ooh. Over there!" Misti pointed to the right and Jordan swerved reflexively in that direction.

"What? What is it?" Jordan asked, looking around.

"I used to dance over there. They must have torn the club down. Now it's just a parking lot. Too bad. It was a real classy place. We got a lot of the guys from the Capitol in there for lunch."

"Representatives? Senators? In a strip club? Hold the presses," Cay said.

"Yeah. You'd think they would have been tending to state business, but no, there they were, right in the middle of the day." Misti crossed her legs and stretched, a sign she was getting bored.

"Noon is the best time to work, you know. A lot of people think you'll get the best tips late at night, but by that time most of them are asleep or so drunk they forget to tip you at all. At noon, they feel kind of frisky, like little boys playing hooky from school, and they tip big."

"Jackson, do your knees hurt you?" Jordan asked. "I see you sort of clutching them. Does the shrapnel still hurt sometimes?"

"No Ma'am. I hardly feel it at all."

"He's clutching his knees, Jordan, for the same reason that Misti is gripping her seatbelt and I am hanging onto the door. Your driving tends to inspire that behavior."

"You don't like my driving, Cay? I'm a perfectly good driver. I can't believe you'd say that. Who tailed Mary Alma Harwick when we were looking for evidence to exonerate Andrea?"

"Who took down a mailbox while just driving along Northside Drive?" Cay asked.

"My van has an awful blind spot. The mailbox thingy was not my fault," Jordan said. "Besides, when you ride with me, I get nervous."

"Lew was going to get me a Hummer because he said I always drove like a was running from the law. He said he'd buy me a pink one." Tears began to trickle down her cheeks at her memory of Lew's thoughtfulness. She grabbed a blue tissue from her bra and wiped her face. "Oh, I forgot to tell you. The coroner's office called, and they released Lew's body. The mortuary is going to pick him up. I scheduled a memorial service for him Saturday morning."

"Wow, Misti, that it a huge piece of news. Does that mean your condo is no longer a crime scene? Can you get back in?" Cay asked.

"Yeah, I guess so," she said, popping her gum.

"Then you can get your make-up case and purse and whatever you had with you the night of your wedding."

"Yeah, right. With all the carrying on, I sort of forgot about it. I'll go back to the condo tomorrow," Misti said. "You guys can come with me, if you want to."

"Oh, we want to," Cay said. "I mean Jordan really wants to, don't you Jordan?"

"Don't I want to what?" Jordan replied. "I'm concentrating up here."

Cay said, "Slow down, Jordan. We have to make a turn here somewhere. There it is, up ahead on the left. Pull through the gates, stay right and get the truck weighed, and then on the way out, they'll weigh it again, and what you owe is based on the difference. Clever, huh?"

"How come you know so much about the dump?" Misti asked.

"I've done my share of rehabbing," Cay answered. "That bungalow of mine in Lullwater pretty much had to be gutted, and I made a lot of trips to the dump. I consider it one of Atlanta's scenic attractions."

Chapter 16

Jordan pulled onto the scale and slid out of the truck. She chatted awhile with the woman in the booth before returning with a yellow piece of paper.

"What was that all about?" Cay asked.

"She likes my ride. I tell you, if you want to meet people, get one of these babies. Everyone wants to strike up a conversation."

"Let's move along," Cay said. "I don't want to spend all day doing this."

"Oh, don't be so grumpy. It won't take long. Eager to get back to the monastery?" Jordan asked raising her eyebrows. She followed the signs to the road around an enormous metal shed. A man waved her toward a bay for unloading, then blew a whistle and gestured for her to stop.

"What is this? First he says go, then it's stop, then it's the whistle." Jordan pressed the button to lower her window.

"He wants you to back in," Jackson said.

"Back in? Is he kidding? How does he expect me to do that?"

"Would you like to switch places and let me do it?" Jackson asked.

"No, of course not," Jordan said. "I can do it. I just have to take my time." She turned the truck around and made a wobbly line, rear end first, toward the bay.

"Jordan, you are too far to the left. You are going to hit your mirror!" Jackson's warning was followed by a scraping noise and an expletive from Jordan.

"One more pass and then I am climbing over the seat and backing it in myself," Cay threatened. "That door must be fifteen feet wide. It's hard to miss."

Jordan more or less aligned the truck on the second try. She backed in slowly, the man with the whistle waving her on as if she were parking a jumbo jet. "See? I did just fine. You guys were just getting me rattled."

"Let's unload this stuff so we can get out of here," Cay said. "Everybody out."

"Gotta get back for a hot date?" Jordan asked. "With a monk, maybe?"

"Jordan, enough. Your record is stuck," Cay said. "It is possible to work with a man not have a sexual relationship, you know.   Men and women can be colleagues."

"Bullshit," Jordan said. "It's always about sex, whether you think it is or not."

"Maybe that is one reason you are so dissatisfied," Cay said, dropping to the pavement from the truck cab.

"Oh, you are a psychiatrist now, are you?"

"Stop arguing," Misti said. "It sounds like the dressing room of the Cheetah II. Bitch, bitch, bitch, all the time."

"There isn't all that much to throw out," Jackson said. "You ladies relax and I'll take care of it."

"Nonsense," Jordan said, "We can use the fresh air and exercise." She sniffed. "Well, the exercise, anyway. Jackson, you throw things down to us and we'll toss them onto the pile."

"Really, I could just throw them straight onto the pile from up here. No problem."

"Hey, look." Cay was pointing a couple of bays over. "What's over there?"

Misti stood on tip toes. "I see what you mean. It looks like a lot of shiny metal things. Are those toaster ovens?"

Jordan squinted and headed in the direction of the glinting metal mound. "There must be a couple of hundred of them, at least. They look brand new. Look, that one even has its cord all wrapped up. I'm going to take a look."

"Hey lady," the whistle man shouted. "It's dangerous to walk around in here. Stay with your truck."

"I just want to see those toaster ovens," Jordan said.

"No scavenging. See the sign? Go back to your truck."

Jordan refused to be put off. "They look like they've never been used," she said. "I volunteer at the Women's Justice Center in Grant Park. We could really use some toaster ovens. Just one, please?" She twisted a red curl around her fingers. The whistle man stood firm.

"I don't want us to get thrown out of the dump," Cay said to Misti. "That would be a new low, even for us."

Cay walked up to the whistle man. "Who left these?" she asked.

"I don't ask who dumps stuff," he said. "I just make sure they don't leave a mess."

Cay thought, *Leave a mess? It's a dump for God's sake.* She said in a solemn tone, "That's a big responsibility. We don't want to cause you any trouble."

"How much could it hurt if we took just one of these?" Jordan said in her sweetest voice. "What's your name, anyway? Mine's Jordan."

"I'm Anthony, and I can't let you do it, Ma'am. I'm the supervisor and I'd lose my job."

"Did I see Jordan wink at the whistle guy? Please say I was wrong." Cay whispered to Misti.

"He's not so bad," Misti said. "I've seen a lot worse. "

"That shouldn't be our standard, Misti," Cay said.

Jordan stepped a little closer to Anthony. "So who did you say left these?"

"I already said I didn't know, Ma'am," Anthony said, taking a step back. "It was just a rental truck, the kind with the big painting on the side of some different part of the country where the truck was from, or some shit like that. This one must have been from Vegas because it had showgirls and dice and that kind of crap painted all over it"

"And he's well spoken, too," Cay said.

"Vegas," Jordan said. "That's odd. That's where you and Lew were married, Misti."

"Yeah. What a crazy coincidence," Misti sniffled a little.

Cay shuddered when she heard *Rave On* by Buddy Holly. It was Jordan's cell phone. She put her finger in one ear to drown out the noise of a front end loader shoving around the mountain of trash.

"Hello, yes, this is Jordan McKeehan. You're shitting me, right? How can you tell?" There was some more conversation then Jordan shouted, "I was right! The damn brakes on my van were cut." She spoke into the phone again. "Listen, if I call the police would you explain this to them? Great, I happen to have a friend on the force. Be expecting a call from Detective Jerry Bongiovanni."

Cay grabbed Jordan's arm. "Jordan, what is it? What's going on?"

"It was the car dealer repair shop. The brake line on my van was cut! The bad news is someone was trying to kill me. The good news is I get to call Jerry." She reached in her purse for her chapstick.

"You know, Jordan, someone may have been trying to harm Misti, not you," Cay said.

"But I get to work it," Jordan said. "Should I cry a little? On Bongiovanni's shoulder, I mean."

"Jordan, are you totally egocentric?" Cay asked.

"Can I ask a dumb question?" Misti looked puzzled.

"Better than anyone I know," said Jordan.

"What's egocentric?"

"Someone who goes after what she wants and isn't ashamed to say so, apparently," Jordan squared her shoulders and climbed into the truck.

Chapter 17

"Trish, Andrea! You guys will never believe this!"

"Whoa, Jordan. Take a deep breath and tell us what's going on." Trish and Andrea were working in the Justice Center kitchen with Isabelle and Mother.

"My van brakes were deliberately cut and that's what caused the accident at Brio! Someone tried to kill me!" Jordan fell into a chair. "I called Jerry on the way here."

"Have you ever ridden with Jordan in a huge truck while she's talking on her cell phone?" Cay asked as she entered the room. "She cut a wide swath, weaving in and out of lanes on I-85. Drivers were swerving, horns blaring. I ducked so no one could see me."

Trish said, "Jordan, that's terrible, about your van I mean. Why would anyone deliberately cut your brakes? What's going on here? Horrible things are happening all around us. The shopkeeper shot on Buford Highway and now Jordan's van sabotaged. Is a pattern in all this?"

"The pattern here is I seem to be bad luck all around," Misti observed.

Ace jumped up on Jackson when he followed Misti in. "Whatever the reason, it looks like you ladies got some security at the right time," he said. "And ladies, just a reminder. That door we just came in wasn't locked, was it?" he asked.

Andrea replied, "That lock is so old it's hard to lock. You have to jiggle the key several times to get it right."

Jordan ignored Andrea and Jackson. "Yes, it's all about you, Misti. It was my brakes that were cut. Turn the spotlight back on me, please. Jerry is going to interview the repair guy at the dealership today."

"Jordan, I wouldn't doubt you cut your own brakes just to have an excuse to call Jerry," Cay said.

"Yeah, like I really know where the brake lines are. I don't even cut my own nails. Manicures, shamicures, any way, what about those toaster ovens?"

"What are you talking about? What is this about toaster ovens?" Trish asked.

"There were a shitload of brand new toaster ovens at the dump." Misti explained. "Jordan wanted to take one, but Captain Dumpster wouldn't let her."

Mother spoke up, We could sure use a couple of those here at the Center. "When we have more residents, we are going to be hard pressed to get quick breakfasts at the same time without more than one toaster oven. Hey, maybe we could give them out as door prizes at the grand opening."

"Well, I'm going back to the dump as soon as it's dark and pick up a few," Jordan folded her arms. "Anyone else wanna go?"

"You're kidding, right?" Trish asked. "That has to be against the law. Isn't it a crime to take things from a county dump?"

"Hell no, I'm not kidding. It's a crime to throw out a couple of hundred brand new Braun toaster ovens. We need them here and I want one for Twelve, when I buy my condo. The new me, the new toaster oven - very symbolic.

Just hope it's not the only thing that gets hot and pops up in my new place."

"Jordan, I frequently ask myself why I hang around with you," Cay said. "It would seem I learned my lesson when you and I had that pot party, if you could call it that."

"And your answer is, life would be so boring without me, right? OK, I'll take that as a 'yes.' Alright then, Cay's going, I'm going..." Jordan looked around the room.

"Count me in," Mother said.

Isabelle looked at her in shock. "Mother, I do not want to have to bail you out of jail. You most certainly are not going."

"Oh be quiet, Isabelle. I'm an old lady. If I don't kick up my heels now, then when? Look at it this way. If I get arrested and you have to bail me out, the dump is only a few hundred yards from the jail. At least you won't be out driving all over town in the middle of the night."

"You've kicked up your heels your whole life," Isabelle said. "I would think it might be time for you to settle down."

"I'll settle down when I'm dead. What is the right thing to wear when stealing from the dump?" Mother asked Jordan.

Jackson quietly left the room, taking Ace with him.

"Well, none of the rest of us are going," said Trish. "And what 'pot party' did you have, Jordan? Was it a kitchen shower for your new condo? Which, by the way, you haven't closed on yet."

"If that is what you want to think," said Jordan.

"Trish, it was one of the worst nights of my life," Cay said. "Jordan came over after leaving a bar and had some pot with her. Her 'teen-aged date' had slipped a little bag into her coat pocket while the bouncer was checking ID's and she didn't know what to do with it."

"So she came to your house for advice? Why you?"

Jordan said, "Because Cay knows everything."

"Oddly enough, I've had a little experience with pot." Cay shrugged. "This was long before you knew me, Trish. My former love, Conrad, used it to relax after working at the hospital clinic. So I still had some of the rolling papers. I guess I kept them for sentimental reasons."

"Yeah, that is the same reason I kept the pot. Sentimental reasons."

Mother said, "I find it relaxes me too."

"Mother!" Isabelle exclaimed. "You're joking and it's not funny at all."

Mother just stared at her.

"What was it like?" Curiosity overruled the illegality for Trish.

Jordan sat up straighter. "Well, after a few puffs, I got hungry. I think they call that the munchies. But I couldn't figure out how to open Cay's refrigerator door. I knew there was food in there, but the logistics of opening the door baffled me. Frankly, I don't like it when I can't be in control. Especially when it comes to food. Cay just giggled and couldn't stop."

Mother interrupted. "How about those toaster ovens? What time are we going? Are we going to wear masks and disguises? A new adventure! I love it." She rubbed her hands together like a kid on Christmas Eve.

"I'd think a sweat suit would work well," Jordan said. "Something dark."

"I can't believe this," Trish said. "You're discussing proper wardrobe to commit a theft? If ya'll insist on returning to the dump tonight, the rest of us have something else to do," Trish said. "Misti, we know it is your birthday, and we want to give you a little party tonight, which means ya'll have to get back here before it gets too late."

"A party? For me? I've never…that is so…" She searched her bra for a tissue.

"Here, dear." Isabelle handed her a box of pink scented tissues. "Mother plans to bake you a cake. It's her specialty."

Mother winked. "I use a secret ingredient that makes all my cakes special."

Isabelle sighed. "Mother we all know you cook with bourbon and sometimes you put it in your cakes."

Trish said, "Since you said you've never had a sleepover, that is what we are going to have, a real girlie slumber party. The Chix brought their pj's so we are all set. Don't peek in the dinning room when you get back. Ladies, make this dumpster caper short, all right?" She looked at Jordan.

"Don't get your designer panties in a wad," Jordan said. "We'll be gone and back before you know it."

Chapter 18

"Tell me again why I'm doing this?" Cay asked. She was clutching her tightly fastened seatbelt strap in the shotgun seat of Jordan's truck as it plummeted southward on I-85 toward the dump.

"Because these toaster ovens are a steal," Jordan said.

"That's very funny. Jordan, you are so funny." Misti paused in her appreciative laughter to pop some Juicy Fruit in her mouth.

Cay did not sound amused, "I hope the police are laughing when they pick us up. What was I thinking?"

"Oh, Cay, nobody is going to pick us up." Jordan flipped down the visor to check her hair in the mirror. "Besides, I think I saw a place to hide the truck near the back fence. We will be in and out of there before you know it."

"Does this thing have a heater?" Cay asked. "My feet are cold."

Jordan turned the heater on to high. "You have on black wool socks, and the little white flashlights are charmingly appropriate, I might add. Seems to me those would keep you warm. Where do you find all these crazy socks?"

"You should surf the web Jordan. Shopping is now a placeless pursuit. These came from The Sock Shop in Savannah, for instance. You know how much I detest going to malls. Man, your heater is hot! I don't need to be fried – just a little warmer will be fine. Misti, I don't know how you can run around with bare legs this time of year. It is really cold out there."

"I never feel the cold. My mom says I ran around naked all the time when I was a little kid, even in the winter."

"The more things change…" Cay said.

"Mind if I play the radio?" Misti asked, reaching over the seat back and punching some buttons. She finally came to a country station that seemed to suit her. She sat back down and began to sing along.

"I'll bet those folks behind us are sorry you found a station," Cay said. "That must have been quite a view."

"I'm going to miss this truck when I have to give it up," Jordan said.

"It's not getting repo'ed is it?" Misti asked, concern in her voice.

"No, nothing like that. Remember? I said it was a loaner. When my van is fixed. it's back to my mom car."

"How is the mom thing going, by the way? What does Michael think of your hair? Have you talked to him about Twelve ?"

"He thinks I'm crazy, but that's nothing new. My son's all wrapped up with looking for colleges and visiting them with his dad. There is a lot of father/son bonding going on right now, and that's good, because there hasn't been a whole hell of a lot for the previous seventeen years. Jim's a fairly good father when he's around."

"Doesn't that beat out excitement?" Cay asked. "Seems to me that men who can be good fathers are hard to find, while the party boys are a dime a dozen. I think you ought to count your blessings."

"That is so true," Misti said. "I never knew my dad. Neither did my mom." She paused. "That was supposed to be a joke, girls. But it was almost true. He took off when I was a baby and mom never heard from him again. I used to think I would find him someday, but that was a dumb idea. He's probably dead or dead drunk now anyway. I think maybe that's one reason why I was so attracted to Lew. He was sort of fatherly. Not in a weird way, but just kind to me and a good listener. You are so lucky your husband even wants to be a father. You don't know."

"My husband died when Isabelle was a teen-ager," Mother said. "I still miss that man. Never could find one good enough to replace him."

Jordan squirmed a little behind the wheel. "I know all of you are right. My brain knows it, but I can't help what I feel inside. You know what I thought the other night? What if I never danced with a man again? What if I died and the last time I danced with a man was at my wedding? I couldn't bear it."

"Then take ballroom dancing, for heavens sake," Cay said. "Or join a tango club. You look like tango material. Watch out for that car in front!" Cay covered her eyes.

"I'll go if you go. It wouldn't hurt you to meet a few men, you know," Jordan said.

"I thought we were talking about dancing. I'll go if you want to dance. I do not consider a tango club a prime place to meet men."

"Why not?" Misti asked. "Latin types are pretty hot, I think."

Cay turned toward the back seat. "In this case dear, one woman's hot is another woman's not. But I appreciate your thoughts on the subject. Don't miss the exit, Jordan. It's the next one."

Mother grinned, still enjoying her memories. "The race track used to be my hunting spot, but I wouldn't recommend it. I got tired of sorting the gambling addicts from the week-end players, so I quit going. I got pretty good betting on the ponies, though. Easier to tell a good horse than a good man."

Misti peered out the truck window. "It's kind of scary down here after dark, isn't it? I wish we had Jackson with us."

Jordan frowned. "Andrea wouldn't let him 'take part in a crime,' as she put it, but we'll be fine. Don't wimp out on me. I'm going to pull into the dirt road over there just outside the dump fence. I think I can park so the view from the road is mostly blocked by the weighing shed."

She jerked the truck over the curb, cut the lights and drove a couple hundred yards along the fence until she found a spot that suited her.

"Turn the truck around and head it out," Cay said.

"Why?"

"Because, Jordan, if we need to make a quick getaway, the truck will be pointed toward the road."

"Hey, have you done this before?" Misti asked.

"No, but I watch a lot of TV. Too much. Go girls, and make it fast." Cay wiped her sweaty hands on the front of her pants. "Mother, you be our lookout. Stay in the truck and blow the horn if you see the cops."

Jordan turned to caution Mother, "Don't turn on your flashlight, the moon is bright enough. Besides we wore black for a good reason."

Cay rolled her eyes and said, "Here I thought I was wearing black because it makes me look slimmer in a line-up. Don't forget these," she said, as she handed Jordan and Misti some black plastic industrial strength trash bags.

Misti and Jordan ran to the break in the fence Jordan spotted when they left the dump earlier in the day. Not really an opening, the fence had settled and the post pulled away from a gate, leaving enough room for a skinny person to squeeze through.

"I don't know," Jordan said, sizing up the width of her hips and the fence opening. "Maybe I was wrong. It looks awfully small."

"I can get through there," Misti said, "You have a pretty big head. I don't know if you can make it or not."

"Remember, I'm from Jersey; it's mostly hair," Jordan said. She took off her leather jacket and handed it to Cay.

"You don't have any Vaseline in the truck, do you?" Misti asked. "It would really help."

"No, no Vaseline. We'll have to do the deed without greasing up. I'll remember it next time."

"You plan on doing this again?" Misti asked. Jordan didn't answer.

After some pushing and colorful expletives, Jordan squeezed through the fence opening. Misti slipped through like an eel. Apparently pole dancing and yoga had been the perfect training for breaking into a government facility.

Jordan and Misti crouched down and crept along the fence until they reached the shadowy berm. They angled around the back of the shed to the bay where they had seen the toaster ovens.

Cay paced up and down next to the truck until the two reappeared, dragging bulging trash bags behind them.

"OK, let's get out of here," Cay whispered. "I've gotta pee." She started heaving the heavy bags into the truck bed.

"Tough luck," Jordan said. "We're going back."

"Don't be greedy, Jordan. C'mon, guys, I want to go. We've been lucky so far. Let's not push it."

"Stop whining and give me more bags, Cay. We'll go when we have enough." Jordan grabbed the bags from Cay's outstretched hand and the two took off back toward the berm.

Cay started pacing again. She ducked when she saw a car on the road, going fast. *I've seen that car go past here before.* There had been very little traffic, but Cay was sure that the same tan Camry had gone down the road just after Misti and Jordan disappeared into the shadows at the rear of the dump. *Tan Camry's are a dime a dozen, but still, what would the odds of two cars just alike going up and down this deserted road at this time of night?*

Misti and Jordan made several more runs. On the last, Jordan was sweating and gasping for air.

"This is hard work. I thought I was in pretty good shape, but this is brutal." They slipped back through the fence.

Cay said. "Pass those through, help me load them and then get in the truck. We're leaving. Now." Cay motioned mother to get in the back set and got in beside her as soon as their loot was on board. "Look! See that tan Camry? I swear that is the third time I have seen it go by."

Jordan said. "Cay, it's dark and that car is going so fast you can't even tell what color it is in this light. Your imagination is working overtime."

The mound of toaster ovens was secured in the back of the truck with a tarp roped down tightly over them. Jordan pulled slowly out onto the road and turned on the headlights once they were on their way. Jordan and Misti were too tired to talk at first, but as the trip back to the Justice Center progressed, they perked up, laughing and recounting their adventure. Cay kept swiveling around in her seat, looking out the back window.

"What do you have, the heebie-jeebies?" Mother asked. "No one is after us. If the cops didn't get us while we were there, they aren't going to get us now."

"It's not the cops I'm worried about," Cay said. "It's the tan Camry three cars back. It has been following us since we got on the interstate."

Mother smiled. "You have to get used to a life of crime. Forget it. I'm anxious to get back to the Center and celebrate with some birthday cake."

"Me, too," Misti said. "A sleep over. How cool is that?"

Jordan said, "Relax, Cay. Picture tomorrow's headlines in the AJC: *Toaster Oven Caper at Fulton County Dump Puzzles Police.* Remember, we only took trash. We should get a medal for recycling or something."

As Jordan took the exit toward the Justice Center. Cay gave a relieved sigh. "I guess you were right. The Camry kept on going," she said. "I'm just not qualified for a life of crime."

Chapter 19

The lock in the back door of the Justice Center clicked with that new sound. Cay entered first, brandishing her Justice Center key. "Good work, one and all," she said. "You remembered to lock the door. Jackson will be proud of you."

Right behind Cay and almost tripping over her, Jordan pushed through the door, with Misti and Mother following. "It was fantastic," Jordan said. "We got a bunch of toaster ovens. I left them in the back of the truck – all but one. You gotta see this." She lifted a Braun toaster oven to be admired.

Trish said, "What do you mean by 'a bunch?' Jordan, we know how shiny objects attract your attention, but you only planned to get one or two. We don't want the Justice Center to become a hot toaster oven dealer, you know."

"We couldn't help it," Mother said. "They were so pretty and it would have been a real crime for them to be turned into scrap. Do you know what a bulldozer would do to their shiny little bodies?"

Isabelle looked stern. "That is a noble sentiment, Mother, but this isn't 'Save the Whales.'"

"But look," Jordan said, putting the toaster oven on the kitchen counter. "How can it be wrong when it feels so right?"

Cay groaned. "That sums up your whole life, Jordan."

Jordan responded, "And your point is…"

Jackson walked into the kitchen, wearing a tool belt. "I feel faint," Jordan said.

Ace was right behind Jackson. He started to wag his tail vigorously and sniffed. "Aw look," Jordan said. "He likes me." Ace went straight past Jordan to the counter where the toaster oven sat. The German Shepherd stood on his hind legs and sniffed some more, then sat down, ears forward, body tense,

"What's with the dog?" Jordan said.

"That's how drug dogs point out drugs," Jackson frowned. "Let me take a look at that." He pulled a screwdriver from his tool belt to open the oven door. He peered at the inside using a little high beam flashlight. "I'd say there's no doubt that drugs, probably cocaine, have been in or around this toaster oven," he said pulling out small pieces of packing material. Ace growled. "Don't handle this toaster any more. You need to call the police and let them take over."

"Shit," Jordan said. "Can't we just wash it out or something? These were not easy to come by! We risked our lives, our clothes, our manicures…"

Cay interrupted, "…our common sense. Jackson's right Jordan. We have to notify the authorities about these ovens in spite of your hard work and sacrifices."

"We'll call the police, but I am going to call Lanier first," Andrea said. "You stole those ovens and it might get awkward, telling the cops how a bunch of drug contaminated toaster ovens came into your possession. Even worse, the possession of the Justice Center. There are enough people in the neighborhood who already think the

Center will be some sort of hotbed for crime. We don't want their protests to begin in earnest. "

"It's late. I think we should have Misti's birthday party," Isabelle said. "Let's get on our pajamas, have ice cream and cake, and bright and early tomorrow morning, Andrea, you can call Lanier."

"Good idea," Cay said. "I'm starving, and there is almost no problem a little cake and ice cream won't fix. The crime has already been committed. The ovens aren't going anywhere tonight. Let's get on with the celebration."

Chapter 20

"I think I'm gonna cry." Misti dabbed at her eyes with a party napkin while Andrea put Care Bears paper plates on the table.

"Don't do that darlin' or you will make the rest of us cry too. Here, put out the cups." Andrea handed Misti pink plastic cups for the Hawaiian Punch.

"No one ever gave me a birthday party, especially not a sleep-over. Y'all have done so much for me, and now this." Misti waved her arms at the balloons and paper streamers. "It's so beautiful, all of it. Getting me Lanier and giving me a place to stay, and the clothes and now a party. I don't know what to say." She dabbed her eyes again.

Andrea smiled. "That's what the Women's Justice Center is all about. Not birthday parties, necessarily, but women helping women. Before long you'll have a good job, with your own place. You'll see. When trouble hits, you think it will stay around forever, but it eventually goes away."

"I guess you're right. Lew's death was such a shock, and then all the crazy stuff that's happened since. The worst part is Lew's killer is still out there."

"Let's think of happier things tonight. Will you be warm enough? I can loan you a robe if you need it."

Andrea eyed Misti's sheer baby doll pajamas with the marabou trim. Andrea's long silk Natori nightgown and peignoir in leopard print with fuchsia piping was scarcely warmer, but at least it was opaque. "Will you please call the others? You can use the intercom. It goes to the bedrooms. It is almost midnight, so let's get on with the party."

Before long, Cay, Trish, Jordan, Isabelle, and Mother trooped into the kitchen.

"Aren't y'all something!" Andrea exclaimed. "Let me get my camera. It's in my bag upstairs. An adult pajama party should be recorded for posterity." Andrea dashed up the back stairs. Trish wore her uniform of designer sleepwear. Tonight it was a Vera Wang cream colored cashmere robe and a simple silk gown. The blue script monogram on the robe matched the blue satin facing on the sleeves. Jordan, not surprisingly, had gone for a vivid red that clashed with her hair. Cay stared at her choice of nighties.

"So? I like big T-shirts," Jordan said. "And red makes me happy. No news there. Move along." Mother and Isabelle were in sensible, floral printed flannel granny gowns.

"The winner of the pajama competition is you, Cay," Andrea said as she returned with her camera.

"There was a contest? I didn't know that," Cay looked around.

"She's kidding," Jordan said. "It's the footies. Really, Cay, where can a grown woman get footie pajamas?"

"I always wear footie pajamas in the winter," Cay sniffed. "My house is cold and my feet freeze. I don't think that's so odd."

"You need to get out more," Jordan said.

"You need a man," Misti said. "Oops, was that rude? I just meant to put your cold feet on."

"I have a dog," Cay said. "She's warm and cuddly, but I still get cold feet."

Andrea grouped everyone around the cake, which Mother decorated in pink sugar roses and purple frosting ribbons, and snapped a few photos.

"I want copies," Jordan said. "You never know when you'll need blackmail. Oops, maybe that works both ways."

"Let's light the candles," Trish said. "I'll get the matches. Is this all the candles you had Andrea? This couldn't be Misti's age."

"No. There are only ten candles there, silly. I won't tell anyone my age. Even Lew didn't know."

"Darn," Trish said, looking in the sideboard drawers. "Only one match. That's all I can find. We better get this right the first time." She handed the box to Andrea. "You should do the honors since you are our hostess."

"I can look in the kitchen for more," Isabelle offered.

"Don't bother," Misti said. "Go for it Andrea. Ten on a match isn't bad." Andrea lit eight candles before the match played out, then lit the last two from another candle, spilling a little wax on the cake.

Everyone burst into *Happy Birthday*. Trish got a picture of Misti aglow in the candle light. As soon as she blew out the candles, Andrea handed Misti a cake knife and the group around the table began passing her their plates.

"Me first," Cay said. "Liberating toasters makes me hungry."

"Getting all those toaster ovens was hard work," Misti said. "A real work-out."

"You mean stealing all those toaster ovens," Andrea said. "We can't keep them."

"Well, they are snug under a tarp in the back of my adorable truck, so we can think about that in the morning."

Jordan said. "OMIGOSH. There I go again. I sound just like Scarlet O'Hara. Now I know I need a trip to Jersey."

"My my, I've missed a lot," Isabelle said. "You all will have to bring me up to date on your adventure."

"Everything waits for the cake," Cay insisted. "Stolen toaster ovens can wait for morning, but birthday cake and ice cream can never wait."

Misti pulled out the spent candles and put them on a paper plate. Then she carefully cut eight slices. "We'll save a piece for Jackson," she said. "I'm glad this is girls only party."

"I wanted to include him," Andrea said, "but I also wanted for us to cut loose and have fun, and our ensembles are hardly appropriate for mixed company."

"Speak for yourself," Misti said. "Dig in." There was silence as everyone started on the chocolate cake with butter cream icing. "Mother, this is amazing. You are really a great cook."

"It is delicious," Andrea said. "What is your secret?"

"If you must know," Mother said, "a little bit of bourbon does wonders."

"Thought that's what you said for scrambled eggs," Jordan said.

"This is so good," Cay said. "Believe me, it's a compliment when I say it's as good as a Publix cake."

Mother said. "Cay, I'll give you some of my recipes. I don't bake much anymore and Isabelle has never been interested."

"It's not that I am uninterested, Mother," Isabelle said a little sharply. "There is too much liquor in all your recipes. It's all right in a fruitcake, but chicken casseroles?"

"Nonsense," Mother replied. "A drop or two of something alcoholic helps everything taste better. The French put booze in everything." She grinned.

Andrea said, "Misti, you have a present to open." Andrea pulled a gift out of the sideboard. "Happy birthday from all of us, Misti," and handed her a large box wrapped in silver paper with pink satin ribbons tied around a nosegay of miniature roses.

Misti's gasp of delight turned to a shriek as the lights went out and left them in total darkness.

"Don't worry," Cay said. "I hate it too, but it's nothing to get upset about. This is an old building. I'll bet it blew a fuse. That happens in my old house in Lullwater all the time."

"It's important not to panic," Trish said. "This is something we can easily fix."

"You're probably right," Andrea said. "But I had the wiring updated when I remodeled, so we could meet the building codes. I don't understand why the lights went out. We don't have very much plugged in right now. It shouldn't do this."

"I hate the dark," Cay said. "Especially when it's this dark. Don't you have any street lights out front?"

"We do. There's a street light right outside, as a matter of fact."

"Then it's off too, because I am looking out your window and the streetlight should be right there," Jordan said, pointing, "and it isn't lit. Maybe the whole neighborhood is out of power. That would make sense, wouldn't it?"

"I want to see my present," Misti whined.

"Hush," Cay said. "Did you all hear that? It was sort of a scraping noise. Downstairs, I think."

"In the basement?" Andrea sounded impatient. "Cay, it was probably the furnace kicking in. It's cold out tonight. You're the one with the footies on. We'll pretend we are big girls, get a flashlight and go look at the fuse box."

"And then what? What if it's not the fuse box?" Misti asked with a quavering voice.

"Then we will wake up Jackson and ask for his help. But we are going to check for ourselves, first. I don't want him to think we are a bunch of whining, whimpering women who can't look after themselves. Now, where's a flashlight?"

"The last time I saw a flashlight was in the attic when you were pulling out some of the junk," Trish said.

"I had it after that, because I needed it when we were rehabbing Jackson's apartment," Andrea said. "I think that's where I left it. I remember putting it in the broom closet. It must still be there."

"You have candles, but we're out of matches. We used the last one for Misti's birthday cake," Trish said. "How can we be so unprepared for an emergency? "

"Ok, everyone, don't be scared," Andrea said "The Justice Center has a burglar alarm. The doors and windows are wired on the first floor, and there are burglar bars on the basement windows."

"I guess the big question is, Andrea, did you set the alarm tonight after everyone came in?" Trish asked.

"Oh, shit."

"My sentiments, exactly," Jordan said.

"We're being silly," Isabelle said. "We should just pick up the phone and call Jackson, tell him to come over here and see what he can do about the lights. After all, lights are security, and you hired him for security, didn't you? And then we can give him some cake and ice cream."

"You're right, Isabelle. Do any of you have your cell phones with you?" Andrea asked. No response. "OK. Now to find the house phone. There is one on the chest in the front hall. Who wants to go with me?"

Almost at once the other six said, "I do."

"Hold hands," Andrea said. "I'll lead." They snaked around the dining room table, felt the Oriental rug give way to the smooth hardwood floor, and were soon gathered in the front hall.

Jordan glanced out the beveled lights on either side of the front door. "Oops, lights are on at your neighbor's houses, Andrea. Call Jackson, right away."

"There is a slight problem," Andrea said. "I don't know his phone number. I have it programmed in my cell."

"Are you shitting me?" Jordan said. "Call information."

Andrea pressed 411. She waited a minute and pressed it again. Trish took the phone away from her and held it to her ear.

"The phone is dead," Trish said. "We can panic now."

Chapter 21

"The front door needs a key to unlock it. We can't get out this way, but no worries. We can go to the kitchen and leave by the back door," Andrea said, "but I think that is overkill."

"Please don't use that word," Misti said.

"My car keys are in the keeper by the kitchen door," Andrea continued. "I may have left my cell on the counter in there, too. It has a good, bright light. If necessary we can lock ourselves in the car and honk outside Jackson's window. Or if you all prefer, we can drive to the police station."

"Wouldn't we be a charming sight at the police station," Trish said.

"Who are you to talk? You could be in a fashion show," Cay said. "I'm dressed like a six year old and Jordan's T-shirt barely covers her rear end."

"Men of all ages have admired my rear end," Jordan retorted.

Andrea said, "Hold that thought, and let's go to the kitchen."

They walked in a stumbling line to the kitchen, feeling the walls as they went. When they reached the back door, they could see the lights on in a house further down the block. Andrea put her hand up to where the key keeper would be. She found its frame and pulled open its magnet latched door.

She groped around, but there were no keys as she expected. The cabinet was empty. Trying not to betray her growing sense of dread, Andrea patted the counter, but no cell phone.

Trish said, "Talk to me, Cuz. What is going on?"

Andrea's voice shook. "There are no keys and no cell phone. Even if we went out the back door, the truck is locked. I guess we could run across the alley to Jackson's apartment, but in the dark, I don't know…"

"Let's think," Cay said. "If we all get crazy we'll make a bad situation worse."

Jordan snapped. "How could it be worse? We are trapped in a pitch black house with no communication with the outside world ."

"I knew stealing those toaster ovens was a bad idea," Cay said. "And what if I was right? What if someone was watching us at the dump and followed us home. I told you I saw the same car pass us three or four times while I was waiting. They've come for their toasters!"

"Don't be ridiculous." Andrea struggled to keep things calm. "Even if Ace was right about the drugs, that isn't reason for someone to track us down. The toaster ovens were in the trash after all. Whoever threw them away didn't want them any more."

"You ladies are wasting your time." The soft, heavily accented voice came from behind them. "You know how the predator cuts the old and weak from the herd because that is the one that lags behind?" A brilliant light suddenly shown on Mother, a piece of duct tape across her mouth. A tall solidly built man was standing behind her, his arm across her throat while the light glinted off a long barrelled gun.

"I am perfectly willing to let her go if I get what I want, but if I don't, she would be very easy to kill. It is all the same to me. I'll get what I want sooner or later."

"Take the toasters! Take them!" Cay was beginning to cry. "We don't want them. It was just a joke. You can have them."

"Toasters? Are you kidding me? What the hell are you talking about. I don't want no stinkin' toasters. I want the key, and the little babe in the short nightie knows where it is."

He shined the light on Misti, who was hiding behind Cay.

"Do you want to give it to me now, or shall I proceed to phase two?"

"Phase two?" Misti asked in a faint voice.

"That's not the question," Cay hissed. "It's 'What key?'"

"Oh, and, uh, what key?"

"Don't play dumb. You're too stupid to carry it off. We know Vasily gave it to you in Vegas. He told us that much. Unfortunately for Vasily and for us, and now for you, he didn't have the endurance we hoped for. He is no longer in a position to spill the peas, as you Americans say."

"Beans. It's beans. Spill the beans," Trish said softly.

"You never let a mistake go, do you?" Jordan said. "Are we just going to stand here like fools? I'm not." With that, she launched herself toward Mother and the man gripping her, knocking them both over backwards. She gave him a sharp upward jab to the nose with the heel of her hand. His gun went flying.

Isabelle jumped in and yanked Mother away, while Trish grabbed his flashlight. Cay wrinkled her nose and picked up the gun with two fingers.

"Hit him, Trish!" Isabelle shouted. "Go for the temple."

Trish closed her eyes and swung the flashlight. The intruder's head snapped to the right. He turned back to face her and she hit him again. This time she connected with a blow across his nose. There was a loud crack as the bone shattered. Blood spurted onto Trish's cashmere robe but the intruder was unconscious.

"Grab him and throw him down the stairs." Isabelle was taking charge with enthusiasm. "We'll lock him in the basement and call the police." Trish handed Cay the light. The rest of them grabbed pieces of his clothing and dragged him to the door to the basement door After a couple of heaves, he went down the stairs head first and they heard him land on the concrete floor. Isabelle spoke first. "Cay, find the fuse box in the pantry."

"Got it," Cay said. Everyone blinked at the brightness when the lights came on.

Isabelle turned to help her mother up. "Are you OK Mother? Did he hurt you? Sit at the kitchen counter and I'll make you some tea."

"I feel sick," Andrea raked shaky fingers through her hair. "Where's Mr. Chanel? Baby, where are you?" Mr. Chanel came creeping from the direction of the dining room, his party hat tilted over one eye. "Oh, sweet puppy, it's all right. Mommy's safe. Everyone's safe. There, there." She cuddled him close to her face, reassuring herself more than him.

"Omigod", Trish said. "What have we just done?" Her knees gave way and she sank to the floor putting her head in her hands.

Misti was breathing deeply. She asked, "Do you think that guy's alive? Can he get out of the basement?"

Jordan fell into a nearby chair. "Shit. I didn't think I had it in me to actually use that stuff I learned in self-defense classes. I don't think there are any doors to the outside in the basement, are there Andrea? Besides, he didn't look too good. Oy, neither do I. Look at all this blood. You can't use bleach on a red T-shirt. Can you?"

"Right now, laundry is the least of our problems. I'll buy you a new T-shirt." Cay sat on a kitchen stool watching Trish start a pot of coffee.

Andrea put Mr. Chanel on the floor. "How did this awful man get in? First thing, let's get Jackson over here fast."

Cay screamed again as she saw a shadow move across the back parking lot. Someone pounded on the back door. As he unlocked the door, they heard Jackson say, "Everything all right in there? The lights were out. What's going on? You all OK?"

Andrea said, "Jackson, thank God. No, we aren't OK. Someone broke in and tried to kill Mother and threatened all of us with a gun. He cut the phone and the lights. It was horrible."

"The scary guy is in the basement," Misti said. "Thanks to Jordan attacking him, we set on him like a pack of crazed Rottweillers. Trish really pounded him good with his own flashlight. Then we threw him down the basement stairs and locked the door." Ace was growling and sniffing along the floor at the bottom of the door.

Speechless, Jackson stared at the group of ladies.

"In all of this, we forgot Mother," Trish said. "Are you all right?"

Mother was perched on a kitchen stool, a silver flask in her hand.

"She's OK," Isabelle said. "She's got her liquor."

"This is just medicinal," Mother said. She raised her flask in a toast. "You never know when you may need a pick-me-up." She screwed the lid on the flask and tucked it back in her nightgown pocket.

Andrea said, "We can't wait any longer. We have to call the police right now. OK, Trish, please bring your cell phone down and make the call. Will somebody please go with her? Jackson?" She pointed at the basement door.

"Nobody goes down there until the cops come. If you beat him up that good, I'm not worried. C'mon, Ace." Ace stood up, still looking attentively at the door.

"What about all those toaster ovens in the back of the truck?" Jordan said. "How are we going to explain those to the cops?"

"The cops will probably never see them," Misti said. "And if they do, so what? They were thrown away. It wasn't like we stole from somebody."

"The police might view them differently," Cay said. "We trespassed on government property and took those toasters. Who knows what charges they could come up with? Don't forget Ace looked at that one toaster and did his drug-dog thing. That combined with a body in the basement? I'd say we could be in a whole heap of trouble. We have to talk to Lanier and let him tell us what to do before we let anybody see those toaster ovens."

"You make a very good point," Jordan said. "Andrea, I'm going to put the truck in your garage. It will be out of sight and no one will poke over there."

"Jordan, I'm right next door. You think they aren't going to look around, 'make the neighborhood safe', that kind of thing?"

"I'll lock the garage," Jordan said. She fished the keys to the truck out of her bag and went out into the cold February night wearing only her red T-shirt and a pair of flip-flops.

Trish dialed 911 with a shaking hand. She tried to be efficient in her instructions to the dispatcher, but found herself forgetting the address and then saying something about a dead man with a foreign accent. Isabelle took the phone from her.

"It will be all right, dear. Let me." With an impressive economy of words, Isabelle gave a brief description of what happened and their location. She handed the cell phone back to Trish. "They should be here right away. We should all just stay calm. That man in the basement mentioned a key. Misti, do you know what he was talking about?"

"Key? Beats the hell outta me."

Cay said, "I think that is exactly what he intended to do."

Trish frowned. "It might be better not to mention anything about the key right now. You can ask Lanier about that too when someone talks to him about the toaster ovens. This episode tonight could become vital in Misti's defense strategy. It appears someone is now after her too."

Cay said, "I wonder if it is the same person who killed Lew?"

Jordan rejoined the group in the kitchen.

"Here's to Jordan," Cay said raising her coffee mug in the air. "That was downright amazing. If you hadn't gone into your Wonder Woman act, who knows what could have happened?"

"Indeed, dear," Mother said. "You saved my life. You are incredibly brave. Where did you learn to do karate?"

"I took some self-defense lessons a while back," Jordan said. "I decided if I was going to get out there and date, I ought to be prepared to take care of myself."

Cay cleared her throat. "I'm going to have a piece of birthday cake. to settle my nerves."

They returned to the dining room and sat around the table to wait for the police to arrive.

"You remember what that guy said, about Vegas?" Misti said.

"I was kind of in a fog," Jordan said. "I didn't think, just reacted."

Misti nodded. "Well he said 'some guy named Vassily gave me a key. I've been thinking that over and the only 'guy' who might have done it was the guy in the blue sequined dress in the ladies room before my wedding. He borrowed my make-up bag, remember me telling you about that? Maybe he put something in it instead of taking something out. My purse with the make-up bag has been in the condo all this time, since it is a crime scene. So, the tape is down as of this morning, just a few hours from now."

"I guess that calls for some serious sleuthing, since you can get back in to your condo," Trish said. "Do you know where your make-up bag is?"

"Probably. I'm not sure," Misti said. "It was just a little thing I carry in my dressy bag, so I guess it is still there. We can go over there later today, if you want."

"We want," Jordan said.

There was a pounding noise coming from the front of the house. Andrea said, "I better let them in, assuming it's the police. Will someone come with me?" Andrea, Cay, and Misti trooped to the front door.

"We're officers from the Atlanta Police Department. You call 911?"

"Thank you for coming so quickly, officers. We've just had a terrifying experience," Andrea began.

Two Atlanta police officers, a woman and a man, both alarmingly young, stood at the door. The young man spoke first.

"Who is this 'we?'" he asked, looking Cay up and down in her footed pajamas. His eyes widened as they stopped on Misti in her nearly transparent nylon baby doll nightie.

"My friends and me." Andrea indicated Cay and Misti. "Some of us are still in the kitchen. Any way, we were just having a birthday party, and all the lights went out. Then this horrible man…"

"Did you know this man?" The female officer interrupted. Andrea noticed she was furiously taking notes.

Cay moved Andrea to the side. "Of course not. None of us had ever seen him before. He had a strange accent. Sort of like a movie bad guy."

"Do you know where he went?" she asked, as sirens blared behind her. Back-up was arriving. The neighborhood was now well illuminated with blue pulsating lights.

Andrea raised her voice to be heard above the noise, "He's in the basement. Jordan knocked him down with a sharp karate punch. Then Trish hit him with his flashlight. Twice. We all helped throw him down the basement stairs then locked the door. He's still there. We don't know if he is dead or alive."

Misti nodded. "We were scared shitless."

Both officers perked up. The male officer spoke into the walkie-talkie on his shoulder. Several police, guns drawn, jumped from their black-and-whites and rushed to the front porch.

"You probably won't need your guns." Misti spoke up again. "The intruder looked pretty dead."

"Follow me," Andrea said. "I'll lead the way to the basement and you can see for yourselves."

The policemen hesitated in the kitchen. They stared at the pajama-clad group and a fierce looking German Shepard growling with his teeth bared. Jackson grabbed Ace's collar and patted him on the head to calm him down.

"You folks stay right here. Who are you?" One of the officers asked Jackson.

Keeping a good grip on Ace's collar, Jackson explained his role at the Justice Center.

"Still have a few kinks to work out, security-wise, I'd say," the officer said with a smirk. "Which door goes to the basement?"

Four policemen, single file, guns drawn, crept down the steps. Trish made a fresh pot of coffee and got more mugs out of the cabinet. Almost immediately, the officers came back upstairs.

"Is he dead?" Misti asked.

"If he is, he isn't dead here. There's nobody down there, Ma'am. There's some blood, and we'll have the Crime Scene Unit give the basement a good going over, but whoever was down there is gone."

"How is that possible?" Andrea asked. "The kitchen door was locked and there are no doors to the outside down there. The windows have bars. How could he…"

"My guess is the coal chute. It wasn't locked, and it looked like there was some blood on it. It's a good way to get in and out of these old buildings."

"What's a coal chute?" Misti whispered to Cay who explained it used to be the place where the coal truck poured in the coal for the furnace.

"What's a furnace?" Misti whispered again.

"Shush. It's not important." Cay snapped.

"OK. We'll dust for prints, take some pictures and get a statement from everybody. We'll leave a squad car out front tonight, but I doubt he'll come back. Probably some guy on drugs needed money and thought you'd have some here. I wish we had his weapon, but there is nothing down there we could find."

Cay perked up. "Oh, but we do have the weapon." She held up the gun in a Ziploc bag as if it were a poisonous snake.

"Any other surprises?" The officer glared at the group. "Better secure that coal chute door in the morning."

"You can be sure of that, Officer," Trish said. "Coffee, anyone?"

Chapter 22

"So, Red, I hear you're a hero. What other secret skills do you have?" Detective Jerry Bongiovanni was holding a cup of Starbucks black coffee. He sat on the living room sofa in the Justice Center.

"I'll get back to you on that," said Jordan. As tired as she was, she couldn't resist a snappy, suggestive comeback. Jordan curled into a club chair, afraid if she sat close to Jerry she would put her head on his chest and cry.

"How do you know about all this? And so early in the morning, too." Jordan felt as if she had just gone to bed, which was close to the truth. First the police were there until four, and then she was too wired to sleep until almost dawn. Now, only a couple of hours later, here was Jerry.

"I have my sources, kiddo. My spies are everywhere. Really, how are you?"

He has the kindest eyes, Jordan thought. *Dark brown puppy-dog eyes. Bedroom eyes. Omigod, get a grip.*

"I'm OK. Just exhausted." Jordan sat up straighter in her chair. "My women's defense class paid off. Bam! I jammed the heel of my hand right into his nose and it must have worked because he was down. Then, Trish gave him a couple of good whacks with his flashlight. That's what knocked him unconscious."

"But you were the first to take him down, right?"

"Well, everyone was just standing around like sheep. There was only one of him and seven of us, so the odds were in our favor."

"Still, it was very brave, Red. Even though I'm proud of you, don't do anything like that again. You could have been seriously hurt, and I'm afraid of how much I'd miss you."

Jordan felt her face growing warm. She wished she looked better. She changed into a white cotton shirt and black pants and threw away her red T-shirt nightie. The sight of the intruder's blood on it would never leave her memory. She was rumpled, without makeup, and her hair was a mess. Jerry didn't seem to care. He was focused on her beautiful blue eyes.

"It's nice seeing you like this, Jerry. Let somebody else do the police business for once. This isn't your territory is it?"

"No, but I wanted to make sure the Chix were OK. I'm going to drop by this precinct on my way back to the 'hood. I know some good guys there, and I want to be sure they take care of you."

"The 'hood?'"

"OK, da'hood."

Jordan laughed. "You call Buckhead da'hood?"

"Hey. It's good to hear you laugh. Don't worry, Red. I'll make sure they get this guy."

"Problem is, it's more than this one episode, isn't it? Jerry, I don't want to get into shop talk, but all this stuff that's been happening: the explosion at the yoga studio, Lew murdered, the guy shot on Buford Highway when Misti was shopping, and my brakes cut at Brio. Now, some thug with a creepy accent breaking into the Justice Center with a gun. He was not looking to rob us, was he? He was looking for something else. He said he was looking for a key, but we don't know what he meant. That was the game changer. It is no longer, 'Did Misti kill Lew?' The real question is: 'Who wants to kill Misti?' I'm right about that, aren't I?"

"As I said, don't worry. You've done your part. You all have been in enough danger. Now stay out of it and let the police figure this out."

"Stay out of it? It's come to us, Jerry, not the other way around."

Detective Bongiovanni's pager buzzed. "Gotta go, Kiddo." He walked over to Jordan's chair, leaned down and gave her a soft kiss on her forehead.

Flustered, Jordan turned it into a joke. "Jerry, this is so sudden."

He put his hand gently on a bruise on her right cheek. "I guess he landed one," he said, leaving his hand there.

"No, I hate to admit it, but I think it was Mother. She took exception to a remark he made about 'the oldest and weakest,' or something like that. In the chaos she got me more than him."

"You be careful, Red," he said. "You know, I like you like this."

"Bruised?"

"No. But very funny. No, I like you without all the makeup and jazzy wardrobe. You really are a beautiful woman, Jordan, and you don't need to hide behind all of that. Your husband is a lucky guy. But I probably have said too much, haven't I?"

"Not at all." *Not nearly enough,* she thought. *I can not remember the last time an attractive man showed a real interest in me, not in just my looks, but the real me.* "I appreciate that Jerry." *I wish I could show you just how much I appreciate it.* "Kind words are always welcome." *But I can tell you what would be even more welcome...*

Jerry's pager started up again.

"I'll let you out," Jordan said, starting to get out of her chair.

"Stay right there. You look too comfortable. I can find the way."

She touched her cheek. *Thank you, Mother. Good thing, my legs are made of spaghetti right now and I couldn't find the front door with a map.*

Andrea came into the room with a cup of coffee just as Jerry was closing the door. "Was that Jerry? What was he doing here so early?"

"Just checking on us. He said he'd talk to the area cops around here. He is such a good guy and you know how I love his Jersey accent." Jordan sighed. "I'm really due for a trip back home. Think I'll call some of the old gang and have a mini-reunion."

"Right,"Andrea raised one eyebrow. "You all reunite more than Peaches and Herb. Before you do anything, you need something to eat. There's coffee, some fruit and several kinds of cereal in the kitchen if you're hungry."

"I think I'll finish my piece of birthday cake. I hardly touched it last night and I sure couldn't eat a piece with Cay after all the excitement. I wrapped mine up and put it in the fridge. Nothing better than cold, day-after birthday cake."

Andrea said, smiling. "You amaze me, Jordan. You eat like a truck driver on steroids, never gain a pound, and now we find out you're Wonder Woman. Those were some pretty fancy moves last night. You probably saved us from being killed."

"You know Andrea, I have been rethinking my life."

"Whoa! Where did that come from?"

"Where did what come from?" Cay looked half-asleep. She had a coffee mug in one hand and Mr. Chanel in the other. "He wants his Mommy," she said as she deposited a wagging Mr. Chanel on Andrea's lap. "Now, what are you all talking about?"

"Jordan was rethinking her life," Andrea said.

Cay said, "A near-death experience can do that to a person."

"I'm serious. Here I am, thirty-nine…"

"Forty, but who's counting," Cay sat on the sofa by Andrea.

Jordan glared at Cay. "As I said, thirty-nine-ish, and I don't think I want what I thought I wanted."

"Huh?" Cay said. "Run that one by me again."

"Well, I thought I wanted my life to change, get something going, pick up the pace a little – more excitement, and now I think I don't want that at all. I'm not sure what I want."

"I don't have a real marriage. I have more of a business partnership with Jim and I want a more complete feeling. It's not that I want an exciting man, I want a man who is excited to be with me, more of a soul mate. I miss being with someone who values my opinion but still pats me on the butt when he passes by. If it wasn't for my son, Michael, I wouldn't have a family and before long he'll graduate from high school and go to college. If I'm not a wife or a full-time mother, who am I?"

"If we all waited for our soul mates to show up, at that rate the population would take a sharp drop, that's for sure," Cay said.

"What's this talk about soul mates," Trish said, coming into the room with several small glasses of orange juice on a tray. "Drink up. Y'all need your vitamin C. Fatigue affects the immune system."

"Yes, mommy," Jordan said, taking a glass. "I was saying what I want is a soul mate, not some flashy guy who drinks too much and stays out too late."

"You can handle that part by yourself, right?" Cay couldn't resist.

"I'll ignore that," Jordan folded her legs underneath her. "I just feel so lost sometimes because I don't think Jim is ever going to change and maybe I'll never have what I consider a good marriage."

"Maybe you won't," Trish said, "but it wouldn't be the end of the world."

Jordan put her empty juice glass back on the tray. "You can say that because you and John had a great marriage before he died. At least you know what it's like to live with the right person."

"John and I loved each other dearly, but was he my soul mate? I don't think so. That wasn't necessarily a bad thing. We can't always look to someone else – especially a man - to make us complete. No one person can meet all of our needs, and that's another good reason to cultivate close friendships with women. All of you have played a very important role in helping me live without John."

Jordan looked at Cay. "Cay, haven't you ever wanted to find the perfect guy? You refuse to go on blind dates, and he isn't going to come to you without effort on your part. Or maybe you have found a guy. Misti says your change in attitude lately is due to a man. It's more than an occasional wedding that you are running off to, isn't it?"

"What attitude? Misti, doesn't know me. I tend to be grumpy in general. I am just not one for bullshitting about my private life, especially when the topic is men." Cay put her coffee cup on a side table. She realized Jordan was genuinely interested in her opinion. She steepled her fingers, thought a minute and continued.

"I thought Conrad was the right person. Some times, I still do. We were so perfect together, we clicked on so many levels. I couldn't imagine anyone else who would be as right. All the time our relationship was falling apart I couldn't believe it. I wanted to fix it so badly I probably just made things worse. I resented his passion for his medical research and I resented the people he researched with, who had his time and attention. Most of all I resented Africa, the guinea worm, his father, and Jimmy Carter."

"Bless your heart. That is a whole lot of resentment for sure," Trish said.

"When it came right down to it, Conrad needed to please his father more than he needed to please me. His father always told Conrad he was the reason he survived the Holocaust: so Conrad could be born and become a great doctor and save people."

"Not much of a guilt-trip there," Jordan said.

"I ask you, what defense did I have against that kind of destiny? Jimmy Carter came along and Conrad got the chance to go with him to Africa and fight Guinea worm disease. That ended our relationship, because I'd always come in second, at best."

"Don't that beat all." Misti wandered into the room still wearing her baby doll nightie.

Cay shook her head and stood. "I was just going to the kitchen for more coffee. Do you want me to get you a refill, Jordan?"

"Yeah. Please," Jordan answered. "Six Splendas and a half cup of half-and-half."

"How could I forget," Cay said. "Anyone else?"

"Sit back down, Cay," Isabelle came into the living room from the kitchen. "We have a brand new tea cart so I decided to use it."

"It's like a rolling bar," Mother said, coming up behind her.

"Anyway, I loaded it up with coffee supplies so no need to go into the kitchen for refills."

Cay settled back into her seat and continued. "Anyway, what I was getting to is I have made a very happy and fulfilling life for myself without a boyfriend or a husband or whatever. I think I am probably more of a whole person than I would have been as Conrad's wife. Maybe I'm rationalizing, but I'm content and don't want to rock the boat."

"I'd marry again," Andrea said, "if I found the right person. Does that sound awful, since Sonny hasn't been dead even a year? I miss being with a man. I'd look for something different this time, though. Because I've changed so much, I'd want someone who shares my new values. When I was married to Sonny, I didn't have any deep thoughts except what to wear to the next party. Now, I want a man with high ideals, whose sole interest isn't in making money. Someone who cares about making a difference in the lives of people in need more than having a wad of Ben Franklins in his pocket."

"And you'd financially support him?" Jordan asked.

"Sure, why not?"

Isabelle stood. "Mother, let me fix you a tub of warm Epsom salts to ease some of your soreness. Come upstairs with me."

"Gin in my orange juice would make me feel a whole lot better quicker," Mother responded but she followed Isabelle out of the room.

"I wonder if Mother puts gin on her Cheerios," Jordan said.

Cay shook her head. "I doubt it, but I'm sure she really does put it in her orange juice. Actually, that doesn't sound bad this morning."

"Not to me," Andrea said. "I think we need to check in the garage and be sure the toaster ovens are still there. Trish, will you call Lanier as soon as possible?"

Mother yelled from upstairs, "I have dibs on two of them."

Chapter 23

Trish called Lanier Poole. "Thanks for talking with me on a Saturday morning, Lanier. You are on speaker phone and I'm at the Justice Center with the LitChix. We have a rather unusual situation and need your advice."

"Trish, I don't believe you've ever called me with a usual situation. The bizarre seems to find the LitChix. What can I help you with today?"

"Last night Jordan, Cay, Mother, and Misti went to the Fulton County dump and 'liberated' twenty-seven brand new Braun toaster ovens. They saw them earlier when they unloaded trash from Andrea's garage apartment."

"I see. That's interesting. But why are you telling me about this? You need a defense attorney for stealing from the county dump?"

Cay spoke loudly, "Lanier, it wasn't my idea. I told them taking those toaster ovens was illegal. I went along because they made me."

Trish frowned at Cay and put her finger to her lips. "It's more complicated than simply taking toaster ovens from the dump. When they got back to the Justice Center, Jackson's dog, Ace, took up the alert position. He is an ex-drug dog. Jackson said there had to be drugs in the ovens for Ace to do that. So... what do we do now?"

"Trish, y'all truly are the most fascinating group of ladies I have ever known. Why don't I have my lab people examine one of them? There's no need to jump to a conclusion until we have concrete information. For now, let's keep this between us. Can you bring me one this morning?"

Trish said, "Of course. Thank you, Lanier. You don't know how much we appreciate you making time for us."

"Did anyone see you all at the dump?"

"I'll let Cay tell you what she thought she saw," Trish said. "Cay?"

"First of all, this dump thing was not my idea," Cay protested again. "I didn't even want a toaster oven."

Jordan shouted. "She's as guilty as the rest of us. Accessory and all that." Grinning smugly, she folded her arms across her chest.

"Cay, we'll work on your defense later," Lanier said.

"OK, well, a tan Camry passed the dump four times while we were there. I thought it was following us back to the Justice Center but it kept going when we got off the interstate. Later though, we had a terrifying experience." Cay looked at Trish who nodded encouragingly.

"A man, a big man, with a heavy accent broke into the Justice Center while we were having a birthday party for Misti. It was awful. He cut the lights and the phone. He held a gun on Mother and threatened the rest of us.

"He said he would kill Mother if Misti didn't hand over some key, but she didn't know about any key. Jordan karate chopped him. Trish knocked him out with his own flashlight then we dragged him to the head of the basement stairs and threw him down. We locked the door and called 911. We all thought he was dead, but the police couldn't find him..." Cay stopped for a breath.

"Good God almighty. You all didn't think to mention this first?"

Jordan spoke up, "He escaped through the coal chute before the cops got here. The Crime Scene Unit people are testing the blood in the basement to try to identify this man. Any way, we all heard him ask Misti about a key. She didn't know what he was talking about. No news flash there."

Trish added, "We thought we should talk to you about our situation before it got more complicated. Do you think there is any relationship between the man with the foreign accent and the toaster ovens? We can't decide."

Lanier tried to suppress his laughter. "Bring one of the toaster ovens into my office and I'll have my lab analyze it. One of my investigators is an ex-cop and I'll get him to contact the precinct to see their take on the intruder. It does seem like an unlikely coincidence that someone would break into the WJC the same night you all went to the dump for your escapade." Lanier paused. "Let's get the Center opened before we have to close it down with half the board in jail.

Trish gasped, "Surely you are joking, Lanier."

"Yes, my dear, at least I think I am."

Trish hung up. "I always feel better after I've spoken to Lanier. So, Chix, it's off to Lanier's office to drop off the toaster oven."

"Can I drive the cute red truck?" Jordan asked.

"Most definitely not," Trish said. "We will take my Land Rover. And I'll drive. Jordan put one of the toaster ovens in a bag. Don't get any more finger prints on it. I'll meet you by the front door in fifteen minutes."

Chapter 24

"What is your latest experiment in the kitchen, Andrea?" Jordan asked. "You are becoming a really good cook." The Chix and Andrea were seated at the dining room table in her newly restored home next door to the Justice Center.

Andrea grinned. "Tonight is very simple. We're having chicken salsa with toppings. It is one of the recipes we will use in our cooking classes at the center."

Cay said, "Jordan, you and I can bring in the food. Andrea, you stay right there. You've done enough."

"Actually we can serve our plates from the kitchen," Andrea said. Andrea led the way for Trish, Cay, and Jordan. They were impressed with the display on the counter. In addition to the casserole of chicken salsa there were side dishes holding sour cream, chopped green onions, sliced black olives, shredded cheese and lettuce.

"OK, add whatever you like to the chicken. There's plenty here." They returned to the dining room with their plates.

Jordan spread her napkin in her lap. "How are you all doing? I'm still freaking out about last night. The idea of the danger we were in puts me over the edge."

Cay said, "I thought that was your hometown, Jordan."

Trish said, "Changing the subject, you've done an amazing job with the Justice Center and your house, Cuz. Your drive and ambition are admirable. In just three short months, you have accomplished the impossible. Moved you and your kids from Buckhead, remodeled the Justice Center building, and gotten the support of the community behind your concept. In a couple more days and we'll be celebrating with the Grand Opening party." She looked at her cousin and beamed.

Andrea smiled back. "Thanks, Trish. I could not have done it without all of you helping me."

"I love the eclectic style of the interior of the Justice Center," Cay said. "Gorgeous oriental rugs from Chateau Soleil, antiques, combined with practical furniture from Ikea. Who would have thought? You have a good eye, Andrea. You've taken an abandoned brick church building and turned it into the perfect facility for meeting these women's needs."

"It works well, doesn't it," Andrea said. "Now, let's discuss the agenda for the larger Board meeting tomorrow while we finish eating."

"You have become such a business woman," Cay said. "I'm impressed."

"Surprisingly, I found out I'm good at this." Andrea glanced at her legal pad. "First, we are keeping to our timetable of opening the bedrooms upstairs to Center residents in one month. Our residents will be referrals from several local program. .The bedrooms can accommodate twenty clients and are fully furnished. You've seen them, and you know they are really charming. A wonderful home for some of my antiques and linens.

"The kitchen staff will come in Tuesday to set up, but they will be here only two days a week on a regular basis. The rest of the time, the residents cook for themselves. Of course we will offer nutrition and cooking classes, and we will have sample menus and meal plans. I won't have junk food in the Center."

"Well, there go my Ding Dongs," Cay said.

"It will be good for all of us," Andrea replied. "Next, I'll give an update on our improved security system, the progress of the medical clinic, and our job training plan."

Andrea went through each topic lovingly and at some length.

"I'm really looking forward to introducing the Board to our new director of Legal Services, Jack Gordon. I've spoken with him on the phone, but I have yet to lay eyes on the man. As you know, Lanier and others strongly recommended him as the best young lawyer in Atlanta working in poverty law."

Jordan said, "Of course he's the only young lawyer working in poverty law, but..."

"Unfortunately, that's close to the truth," Andrea said. "We have funding for him to supervise our legal issues for the rest of the year thanks to some generous donations by board members. We plan to support his position by grants after that. Of course a number of lawyers will volunteer on individual cases *pro bono.* Apparently working with Jack is quite an attraction, so we have a good list to draw from."

Jordan said, "I already have quite an attraction to him. I Googled him and he's a hunk. A little altruistic for me, but hey, variety is the spice, right?"

Andrea cleared her throat and continued down her list, stopping briefly to take a bite of her chicken. She finally came to her last item, volunteers.

"As I have told you, this is the most important category to me. We can have a wonderful plan for a medical clinic, legal aid, day care, job training, but we can't do one thing without volunteers. I don't mean just the professionals who give their time. I mean community people who show up regularly and work where needed.

"Cay, I realize you have a full-time career, so I am hoping you will serve on the Board, organize our donated books and volunteer when you can. Jordan..."

"Wait, wait, wait. I have a full-time career, too," said Jordan.

"OK, what exactly do you do?" asked Andrea.

"Maintenance work: manicures, pedicures, shopping, weight training, self-defense classes, going out to eat, visiting Jersey. I'm my own industry."

"Get over yourself, Jordan," Cay said.

Trish leaned forward. "Jordan, why don't you help Isabelle with the financial aspects of the Center? After all you have knowledge in that area, and I think it is wise to have more than one person keep the books. You and Isabelle work together nicely and have different skills to bring to the tasks."

"OK, but this may cut in to my nap time."

Andrea returned to her agenda. "Trish, I was hoping that you would co-ordinate the volunteers. Somehow you always make people feel good about helping others, especially without pay."

"I would love to help with that task, Cuz. Carolyn Luesing has agreed to organize all the social graces classes: interviewing skills, telephone etiquette, dining, proper introductions of people, etc.. She is so talented in this area. Betty Botts will head up our gallery, Art and Soul, and will also teach painting classes. Everything created will be sold in the shop and part of the profits will defray expenses, but most of the money collected will be used to give the artists some income.

"Of course we will also have volunteers organizing fund raisers throughout the year. This money will pay for various job training in beauty schools, secretarial schools, and goodness, lots more. I'll be working with volunteers in that area as well. I am very gratified how many people are willing to help women turn their lives around."

Jordan stood up. "OK then, meeting adjourned. Turn on the TV. I brought the DVD of Season One of *Desperate Housewives*."

Chapter 25

As Trish maneuvered her Land Rover around a pothole on Marietta Street, Jordan said, "With all the real estate development downtown I wonder why Lew and Misti's condo building is empty."

"Beats me," Misti said.

"Where are you going to park?" Cay asked, as they approached the featureless cement building.

"I think you have your choice," Jordan said. "The street is almost deserted. I guess we'll have to feed a meter."

"Lew had a couple of those hoodie things that go over parking meters. There's one over there." Mitsi pointed to the first meter around the corner. "See. Something on the hood says loading zone, only something or other allowed – and has the name M. Hozk and Company. It's the same name Lew used on our door buzzer. I never paid much attention. Lew's business was way too complicated for me. Park here."

"We won't be here long. This will be short, right?" Cay said. "I don't like lonely, fortress -like buildings in the middle of rubble strewn vacant lots. Call me silly."

"You aren't getting cold feet, are you?" Jordan asked. "Oh, I forgot, your feet are always cold. Hence the socks. Nice black socks with purple keys today, by the way."

"I always dress for the occasion," Cay huffed.

The four approached the chrome front door recessed into the ribbed concrete façade. There were no windows in the front which extended up for fifty feet at least. Only the door intruded on the austere entryway.

"Intimidating," Trish said. The name plates over the intercom buzzers were empty except for the top floor, which was labeled M. Hozk .

"What gives with the name?" Jordan asked.

"I dunno. I guess Lew just wanted privacy," Misti said. "I never asked. In fact, I never realized how much I didn't know until you all started asking me so many questions."

Trish made a funny sound and began coughing.

"Honey, are you OK?" Jordan asked, patting her on the back. "Can you breathe?"

Trish reached into her purse and got a monogrammed linen handkerchief. She blew her nose and wiped her eyes. " OK. Yes, I'm good to go now. Sorry for the interruption." She took out an oversized keychain with a sparkling rhinestone pink bunny on it.

"There is only one key on this keychain you gave me, Misti," Trish said, " and I assume it's for the condo and not the front door, since it looks like an elevator key. How do we get in?"

"Duh, you open the door." Misti pushed the bronze-toned lever down and the door opened.

"Great security," Jordan said. "The front door isn't even locked."

The Chix entered an empty lobby illuminated only by a skylight. They glanced up automatically. A shaft of pale sunlight gave a shine to the polished concrete floor. They were surrounded by featureless walls.

"Cozy," Jordan said.

Trish walked to the elevator in the central core, and pushed the button. The door opened immediately.

"Do you think it's safe to get in there?" Cay asked, peering all around in the dimly lit chrome box.

"Just get in," Jordan gave her a nudge.

There were no buttons to push for the floors, only four small round ports for inserting a key.

Jordan said, "Since there are only four, it must be one condo per floor. Is that right Misti?"

Misti nodded and put a stick of Juicy Fruit in her mouth.

"My word, that makes them awfully big condos," Trish said. "Here goes." She put the key in the port for the fourth floor. The elevator made a slight noise and jerked upward. It took nearly a minute for it to halt and the door to open.

"Shit! This thing is so slow. No whiplash for us," Jordan said. "This would drive me crazy." She pulled out a chapstick and quickly passed it over her lips. "Is it always this slow?" she asked Misti.

"Yeah. I asked Lew about that, because everything else seemed really modern. I don't think he ever answered me. A lot of time his mind was just out there, ya know? Thinking about business and not listening to me. Like a lot of men."

The door opened into Misti's condo foyer. The Chix had reactions very similar to Bongiovanni and Morrow's a few days earlier.

"Not bad," Jordan stepped into the foyer. "Not bad at all. Amazing, actually."

"I was expecting something quite different," Trish said. A pin spot accented an attenuated Giacometti sculpture, and the Georgia O'Keefe lily painting glowed in the light.

"I'm blown away," Cay said, "and we're only in the entry hall." Entering the living room through an archway, she said, "I'll be. There is some amazing art on these walls. Are these copies?" She walked closer to the first one, then stepped back to gaze around the room. "They couldn't be the real thing. Kandinskys...Warhols... Pollocks...a who's who of Modern art. These have to be reproductions, excellent reproductions. What do you all think?"

Jordan put her hands on her hips, "I think the art, real or not, combined with the classic furnishings, is a good look. Really good. In fact, extremely tasteful."

"Damned if I know if they are real," Misti said. "I don't know one painter from the other, that's for sure. They made Lew happy, so it was fine with me. He said they were good investments. I'd probably have picked some I saw at Target, but he liked this modern shit."

Taking Trish aside, Jordan whispered, "What the hell did Lew do for a living, anyway? He couldn't have made this much dough in low-end real estate foreclosures."

"Good question," Trish answered. "I guess we need to ask Misti, although she doesn't seem to know much about him."

"She doesn't seem to know much, period."

Raising her voice, Trish said, "OK, let's get started looking around."

"What are we looking for again?" Cay asked. "Besides Misti's make-up bag and the mysterious key."

"I have no idea," Trish replied. "I guess anything that proves Misti didn't kill Lew."

"Oh, well that's easy," Cay said sarcastically. "This is a huge-ass condo packed with a lot of stuff. The cops, the CSU and the GBI have been all over the place. Do we really think we can find something they missed? I want to help you, Misti, but this seems hopeless."

Trish started moving around methodically. "OK. Let's do this task one thing at a time. Closely examine one chair, one picture frame, one lamp. Do it in small increments. We may uncover something the police thought was unimportant."

They started at the front door and began to work their way around, turning over sofa cushions, moving chairs, peeking behind paintings.

"Hey, look at this." Cay was running her finger across the spines of books in the bookcase. "Misti, you must have half a dozen scrapbooks here, all leather bound. Pretty classy. I love leather bindings." She pulled one out and sniffed it. "I could get high smelling leather." She began to leaf through it.

"Wow. Misti, you were a headliner. It looks like Vegas. Was it? The Playboy Club? Here's a picture of you in a bunny costume. I thought you had never been to Vegas until you and Lew..."

Misti jerked the book from Cay's hands. "This is private, Cay. Thanks for your help, but that part of my life is over and I don't want anyone poking into it. It was a long time ago, All right?"

"Sorry," Cay raised her hands in surrender. "Just trying to help."

"It doesn't matter, ladies," Trish said. "We don't need to be looking at scrapbooks when there is so much else that needs our attention."

Misti put the scrapbook on a club chair and added several others, similarly bound. "These go with me," she said. "There's a photo of Lew in one of them that I want for his memorial service."

"I think this desktop rolls up," Jordan said, "but I can't move it. It's probably locked." A sleekly modern Herman Miller version of the old roll top desk was positioned on the diagonal in the front right corner of the room. "I could probably pop the lock if I had a knife."

"Fresh out," Cay said. "Misti, do you know if there is a key for this desk?"

Misti frowned. "No."

"'No' what," Cay said. "'No' there's no key, 'No,' you don't know?" Cay's voice betrayed her increasing annoyance with Misti,

"No problem Misti. Cay, get a knife from the kitchen," Trish said.

"Me? By myself? Are you kidding?" Cay's eyes widened.

"Oh my goodness. Jordan, go with her, please. You are our martial arts expert."

"It's not martial arts, it's self defense, and you both should take the class."

"We'll sign up next week. Right now, you go first, Jordan, in case there are any bad guys in there. Don't worry, I'll be right behind you,"

.   Trish was examining a blue and white melon jar, it's lid fixed tightly in place, when Jordan and Cay rushed back into the living room.

"If you think the living room is something, you have to see the kitchen," Jordan said. "Poggen Pol. A quarter of a million dollars invested in there at least, and that's just the cabinets. Oy,vey, the stove! When was the last time you saw a twenty thousand dollar stove?" Jordan was out of breath with the glories she had seen.

Cay followed close behind her. "Who was this guy, Lew, anyway? I don't think Misti could possibly know what this condo and everything in it is worth. Oh, here's a knife and a pry-up thingie from a drawer."

"I am beginning to have serious doubts about Misti," Cay said, waiting until Misti was in the rear hall leading to the master bedroom. "Is it possible for her to really be that dumb? Everyone is running around doing everything for her, and still there are little things. Those pictures I saw were of Vegas, I'm certain, and yet she says she went there the first time to get married. And she sort of looked different…"

"How 'different?'" Jordan asked.

"I don't know. The picture of her sort of creeped me out." Cay said.

"But everything creeps you out," Jordan said. "If you want to be creeped out, look at pictures of anyone us a few years ago. When was the last time you were there? How would you know what Vegas looks like?"

"That's not the point. I have been there, and it was Vegas."

"It could have been a backdrop of some kind," Trish shook her head. "There is no way you could tell from an old photo. Give me the knife and let's get on with it. We came to sleuth, so let's stay focused. Misti doesn't have to be your best friend for us to help her. Cay, the problem is you are so smart most people seem dumb to you. And if they really are sort of dumb, well, they are just off your radar." Trish slipped the knife blade under the edge where the roll top met the desk, wiggled it around and finally pried the top free.

"Oh, I hated to do that," she said. "Especially with a George Jensen knife." She slid the top back on its track until it was fully open. She looked in several small drawers and patted the surfaces. "Shoot. Nothing unusual here. Nothing at all." Frustrated, she hit the side wall of one of the drawers.

"Wait a minute. This one moved. I think it is a secret compartment." She gave it another push and slid it backward. "I can feel something in here." She pulled her hand out holding three keys similar to the one that fit in the elevator port. "What do you know. Could one of these be the key that horrible man was looking for?"

"Do you think they unlock the other condos in the building?" Jordan peered over Trish's shoulder. "They look like Misti's key to this place. Do you think Misti would know?"

"These keys prove my point. It seems like there is an amazing amount Misti doesn't know." Cay was frowning. "Are you guys paying attention to all these holes in her story?"

Trish took the keys and went down the hall in the same direction as Misti. "Misti," she called. "Misti?" She pushed open a tall door into the master bedroom. Misti was sitting on the edge of the bed, head bowed. "Darling, are you all right?"

"Lew was killed in this room, and it's getting to me," Misti said.

"Of course," Trish said. She sat on the edge of the bed and put her arm around Misti's shoulders. "We should have been more sensitive. I am so sorry."

Misti shrugged and straightened her shoulders. "I found my purse, and the make-up case, the one I took with me to Vegas. Now I think I'd just like to get out of here. We can open it later, can't we?"

"Sure we can. Let's go back to the living room. I found three more keys, like the one that runs the elevator to your condo. Do you know what they mean? We can talk about it in the living room with Cay and Jordan." Trish stood. "Ready to go? Do you feel OK?"

"Yeah, I bounce back pretty quick," Misti said. "I'm ready." She gave her short skirt a tug, looked around the bedroom, and led the way back to the living room. Trish could swear there was almost a spring in her step.

Chapter 26

"Do we know which floor each key unlocks?" Cay asked. They were crowded into in the elevator, Misti burdened by the leather-bound scrapbooks. "What if we walk in on somebody?"

"I don't think that will be a problem. I told you I've never seen anyone else here," Misti said.

Trish tried one key in the second port in the front wall of the elevator. It went in but wouldn't turn. Another port yielded the same result. With the third attempt the elevator gave a little lurch and slowly started downward. After what seemed like an eternity, it stopped and the door opened. Trish flipped a switch to the right of the elevator door. Overhead fluorescent lights came on. They entered a cavernous space with exposed pipes and cement floor.

"Holy shit," Jordan said. "Well, this is an austere look."

The room contained a mountain of rectangular cardboard boxes, each with a Braun toaster oven pictured on the side. "Would you look at those!" said Trish. "Empty boxes here, toaster ovens at the dump. Anybody else see a connection?"

"What are those machines over there against the wall?" Cay asked. "They look like presses or molds." She walked over to one of them and picked up some white powder on the table tops under the machinery. "Time to go," Cay said. "This is too strange for me."

"Hold on a minute. I'm taking a box with me," Trish said. "One of these has to go to Lanier, too, and fast. Misti do you know anything about this machinery? Do you have any idea what was being made out of white powder in this condo?"

Misti shook her head looking down at the floor. A tear rolled down her cheek.

"Maybe Jerry will know what all this stuff means," Jordan said. "I'm an eyewitness. I could tell him all about it." She pulled out her cell phone.

Cay grabbed Jordan's jacket sleeve. "Stop, Jordan. Let's put this in perspective. Oh, yeah, the old toaster box scam. Cops have seen it a million times. C'mon. I am leaving. Now! Move it everybody!"

Trish grabbed one of the boxes. "Not a word to Jerry or any other policeman until Lanier sees this first. Just for self-protection."

Misti had been quiet until now. "Well, the cops can't say we broke and entered, can they? The keys were in my condo ."

Trish asked, "Misti are you sure you didn't know about these keys before today? You can tell us. We won't be mad. We are just trying to get to the truth to exonerate you."

"I swear I didn't know anything about that secret drawer. I told you Lew was very private. He didn't talk about his life before he met me, and I respected that. I didn't ask questions because I didn't care. He was a good guy, a real gentleman, and that's all that mattered to me."

"Do you think Lew owned this condo, too? He must have. In fact, maybe he owned the entire building. That would explain why it is empty." Trish said as they got back into the elevator.

"I am tired of speculating," Cay said. "I'll give you this, Trish. You make Sherlock Holmes seem like a rank amateur, but I need a break and I'm hungry."

"I'm sure Mother has some goodies in the fridge for us," Trish said. "Let's try to get to the car without being noticed."

At the the front door, Trish asked Cay to peek out and see if anyone was on the nearby streets. "How did I get the look-out job?" she asked.

"Misti and Jordan are too conspicuous, and I've got a big box in my hands," Trish said.

"Well, God only knows you aren't noticeable," Cay shook her head. "Sorry, I meant with the beige and all."

Sticking her head out then stepping back, she said, "It all looks OK to me. No walkers, a few cars. How would I know if one of them were suspicious?"

"You thought that Camry was pretty suspicious the other night, and you were right. We've learned to trust your instincts." Jordan said.

Cay looked out the door again. "No Camrys, no one on the street. OK. Let's go."

They went to Trish's Land Rover at a brisk pace, nearly tumbling into it in their nervousness.

"Man the torpedoes and full steam ahead," Misti said with a nervous giggle.

"Amen," Cay said. "I want to get out of here."

As they pulled away from the curb, Trish said, "Wasn't there some kind of hood on the meter when we parked here? A 'loading zone'or 'reserved' sign or something?"

"Yeah," Misti looked back at the curb. "That was the way Lew arranged for us to park since there was no garage or lot. Oh, Jesus. It was gone, wasn't it? Why would somebody steal one of those? Anyone want gum?"

Trish reached into her glove compartment and pulled out a baby Ruth.

"Floor it!" Cay shouted. "I am not going down for a parking ticket."

Jordan laughed. "Yeah, that's how they caught the Son of Sam."

Chapter 27

"Jordan, I need to talk to you. Right now," Trish said, as soon as they were back inside the Justice Center. Cay and Misti headed to the kitchen to tell Andrea, Mother and Isabelle what they found at Lew and Misti's condo.

"Is it about Twelve? Say 'It's about Twelve.' Please."

"It's about Twelve," Trish said.

"Thank you, thank you," Jordan said. "We can go in the library. It's quiet."

Jordan skipped down the hall to the library and made herself comfortable in a worn leather club chair. "So, tell me, tell me, tell me." Jordan flashed a cocky grin.

"This is not good news, so please don't get your hopes up," Trish said as she shut the door behind her.

"No!" Jordan made a face. "I will not let this dream fall through. I am tired of being disappointed."

"This is the story, as much as I can make it out," Trish said. "Another real estate agent is now handling the listing at Twelve, since Peter Grimm is 'unavailable,' as they put it. I called her and made some inquiries, just to let her know that under the right terms, I might have a buyer. When I asked her who the seller was, she hemmed and hawed around and told me it was a corporate owner but the condo had never been used. The company held it a couple of months and then put it back on the market."

"That doesn't sound bad to me," Jordan said. "Pretty usual, I would think. It's called 'flipping' and I do that a lot in my real estate investments. What's the problem?"

"You're right, and it didn't trigger any alarm bells until today when I saw the name plate at Misti's condo. M. Hozk."

"Ok, so what's that? Czech? Lithuanian? Something Eastern European maybe. It is probably a common name in Jersey."

"It's not where it's from, Jordan. Make the connection. The name above the intercom on Misti's door and the name of Twelve's owner are the same. There are so many possibilities my head is swimming, and none of them are legitimate. We suspect Lew Cannon, or whoever he was, possibly owned their entire building."

Trish started to pace. "Why did he use the name M. Hozk on the nameplate to his and Misti's condo? Was the name M. Hozk a front for some of Lew's real estate investments? What if he was into the drug business? Was he using M. Hozk to launder money for some illegal activity? Did Lew also own the condo at Twelve and use Peter Grimm as his agent of record? Where is Peter Grimm now? Jordan, there are too many unanswered questions and I can not recommend you buy this place. In fact, I'd beg you not to."

"Trish, this is a great bargaining chip for us. Use this to drive the price way down," Jordan said.

"Have you not been listening? What if all this convoluted ownerships mean those condos were bought with illegal funds or drug money? If the federal government gets involved, they could seize all Lew's assets. For God's sake, you would be out a whole lot of money if you bought that condo at Twelve."

"But if he wasn't and they don't, then I wouldn't," Jordan said.

"Jordan, I love you dearly, but I cannot in good conscience let you go through with this transaction. I've been worried about you buying this condo since Peter Grimm failed to contact us. I located another comparable unit in Twelve for sale that has a respectable title and with your permission, I'll call that agent for you."

"Oh, thank you Trish. As long as it exactly like the one I love. Do you think it's too late to call today?"

Chapter 28

Andrea popped her head into the kitchen and asked Misti to join her in her office. After they were seated she handed her a tan envelope. "This came in the mail while you were gone and I thought you might want to open it right away. From the return address, it is from the coroner's office."

Misti's hands shook as she tore the envelope open. "It shouldn't hold any surprises. We know what killed my poor Bunny Boy." She read a bit then handed it to Andrea. "Will you read this please? "I'm too upset to make sense of it."

Andrea scanned it, looked at the findings, and read it again. "This isn't so easy to decipher, but the coroner determined Lew was killed by a blow to the head with a heavy object, in keeping with the evidence that he was struck by a twelve pound bowling ball."

"Duh," Misti said. "I like heavy balls."

"There are a couple of things written down here." Andrea pointed to a few lines of text toward the bottom of the page. "Lew was wearing a human hair toupee, and brown non-prescription contact lenses. I guess that would be a surprise, wouldn't it?" Andrea looked up.

'I did see a wig when I found him, but I was so confused, I guess it didn't register. I thought maybe his murderer dropped it. I didn't get it at all at the time, I was too shocked, Anything else?"

"You remember Lanier said there was something on Lew's face they were going to analyze? Well, it was saliva. Human saliva was found on his left cheek and in his left ear. It was from a male, but it wasn't Lew's ."

"What? Spit? From a guy? My Lew was not queer. Not that I have anything against queers, but he wasn't one."

"Whatever he was, the coroner's report means there was probably someone else in the apartment while you in the shower. A man. A man who may well have killed Lew. Lanier will be thrilled to get a copy of this. It should go a long way to proving you didn't kill Lew."

"This is so confusing. Tell everybody we'll look in the make-up case later. I have to crash for a while." She got up and ran upstairs to her bedroom and closed the door.

"Well, that was a great move," Andrea said aloud.

"Talking to yourself?" Trish stopped in the office doorway when she heard Misti's door slam. "Is everything all right?"

"No, it isn't." Andrea said. "I got Misti more upset than she already is, and with Lewis's memorial service coming up soon. Here." She handed Trish the coroner's report. They walked together into the living room to join Cay and Jordan. Trish passed the report to the other Chix. Jordan read over Cay's shoulder.

"What the hell does this mean?" Jordan asked.

Andrea continued, "According to Misti, Lew didn't a wig, and the saliva thing is just plain disturbing. Was Lew having some kind of homosexual encounter after Misti left for the gym, and it ended in murder? Was he living a double life? Married, but gay, too?"

"I haven't said anything about this to anyone but Jordan," Trish said, "but Lew does seem to have a double business identity for sure. I've been waiting for the detectives or Lanier to say something concrete before getting Misti even more worked up. While I was researching that condo at Twelve for Jordan, I ran into information that leads me to believe that Lew Cannon used the name M. Hozk as a front for his business deals."

Jordan brightened. "Goody. Maybe Lew was dressing up in a wig and contacts to go out as M. Hozk."

"Oh, my God," Andrea said. "You're right. Dirty money may be the motive for someone else killing Lew. The murderer didn't know Misti was in the apartment and when he heard the shower, he fled. Of course that doesn't explain the bowling ball story," Andrea slumped in her desk chair.

"It could have been that he was searching for the keys we found. He thought it might be in a finger hole of one of the bowling balls, and was surprised by Lew messing around in his closet and bam!" Cay was starting to get creative with the murder scenario standing up and waving her arms. "The bad guy did a couple of things to look like the bowling ball was set up to hit Lew and voila, it cast the spotlight on Misti as a murderer."

"Whatever," said Jordan, sounding unconvinced.

Andrea said, "Poor Misti, no matter what, she's going to be left with nothing."

"Well, not quite," Trish said. "I did find out the condo she and Lew lived in is in her name, as well as the furnishings, the art and the rest of the building. The name M. Hozk was one Lew used, but you can bet his role in the company is deeply buried. However, the title to their condo is clear. It was bought with cash and put it in her name. I checked the records in the Fulton County Court House."

Trish stood and busied herself fluffing throw pillows on the chairs and sofa. "I expect all of this is really giving Lanier's researchers and the cops fits. Maybe that is why it is taking them so long to catch on. Of course there is the question of drugs and all that machinery in the condo below Misti's. If Misti just owns the real estate, she could be in a whole lot of trouble, because it is her duty to know. That's the law for you. And if she actually knows what is going on there, well, it would be life in the federal pen, I would think."

"This is awful," Cay said. "This is so much more than murder. Was Lew some kind of drug dealer or Mafioso or something? Would that truck at the dump mean there is a Vegas connection? The killer or killers must think Misti knows too much. Seems to me Lew's murderer is now looking for her. This could be huge. A federal case for sure."

"Misti keeps saying she doesn't know a thing, not that the mob would believe her," Trish said. "How do we know they are not right?"

"I don't believe Misti knows anything," Andrea said.

"That's for sure." Jordan said. "What, why are you all making faces? I was being agreeable for once. "

"As I was saying," Andrea continued, "I think she wandered into an awful situation without any idea of what was going on. This is dangerous for all of us. No wonder we had an intruder. We need to find out what was passed to Misti in Vegas. This danger she's in seems to have started with her wedding in Vegas. Ask Mother and Isabelle to join us in the living room. As soon as Misti comes downstairs, let's open up her bag take a look."

Chapter 29

Misti dumped the contents of her purple sequined make-up bag onto the living room coffee table. Everyone gathered round her and looked at each item: an eyeliner, iridescent blue eye shadow, an eyebrow pencil, tweezers, gum, false eyelashes, glue, a small sharpener for the cosmetic pencils, a compact containing glittery gold powder, a fat brush for the powder, two kinds of lip gloss, and Q-tips. There was one non-cosmetic item: a blue plastic oval, about one inch long.

"You pack a lot in a cosmetic bag, that's for sure," Cay said. "That's more makeup than I've ever owned…in my whole life."

"This is just my emergency bag," Misti said.

"Is there anything there you don't recognize?" Andrea asked.

"What is this, a quiz show? Of course there is. This little fucker." Misti held up the blue oval between her thumb and forefinger. "Looks like one of those birth control thing-ies."

"That looks like a flash drive," Isabelle said. "May I look at it please?" She held out her hand.

"I wish I weren't so dumb about computers," Andrea said.

"Oh, my dear, you could learn in no time," Isabelle said. "I could teach you if you want. But, that isn't important now." She squinted and turned the object over in her hand. "This is a USB key." "Maybe this is what that man was talking about when he kept asking for 'the key' the other night."

"Unless it was the condo keys," Jordan said.

"That could be true, too. We'll just have to put this into a computer and see what we find out. Shall we go to the office?"

The group rushed to the office, stopped by the locked door.

"I take my responsibility very seriously," Isabelle said. "Security at all times." She took a key ring out of her pocket and opened the office door. "Now, let's try this one," she said, choosing the newest computer. Everyone crowded around the flat screen. Isabelle put the key into the port. A sharply defined image popped into view. It was a list, written in the Cyrillic alphabet.

"Well shit," Jordan said. "That's not going to help much unless one of us speaks Russian."

"Well, I do, a little," Isabelle said, "but only a little. Sonny's international business dealings, you know. However, Mother is better than I am. Russians do love to gamble. She's met so many nice gentlemen through her bookie."

"Isabelle, you two never cease amaze me," Trish said. "We can all read the numbers. We just don't know what they mean."

"I will have to study those for a bit. They aren't all in dollars. There are a lot of different currencies here. I see pounds, zlotys, Euros, yen - it seems quite extensive. These are definitely financial records, and they must hold a pretty big secret for someone to want it so badly." Isabelle put on her glasses and stared even more intently at the screen. She scrolled through the documents, pages and pages of numbers and lists.

"There are account numbers, names, the names of some cities. This will take awhile." Isabelle settled herself in the desk chair. Her cheeks were pink and her eyes shone. "I love a challenge, especially a financial one. This is going to be a very exciting evening."

Chapter 30

"Thank you all for coming with me. You're my only family now." Misti sniffled into a tissue. "It's been a hell of a time, hasn't it? I wish things would calm down and life would be more normal, whatever that is." They got out of Andrea's car in the Restful Hills Memorial Gardens parking lot, which was neither restful nor hilly, having its hills shorn level by Interstate 85.

Andrea replied, "Of course we're here for you Misti. You'll get through this, but it is a tough time. I know."

The LitChix, Andrea, Mother, Isabelle and Misti went through the funeral home's double doors and were met by the funeral director.

"The Cannon memorial service please," Trish said. They were shown into a small room. Burgundy fabric covered the opposite wall. An Oriental-patterned runner led down the only aisle.

"This is lovely," Trish said looking around.

"Dignified," Misti whispered. "Lew would have liked it. He liked the finer things." The Chix exchanged a knowing look.

Several flower arrangements were on the table at the front: a vase of white lilies from the Justice Center, a bouquet of dried pink miniature roses, and a multicolored wreath on a stand.

"Who are those flowers from?" Cay whispered back, pointing to the wreath. They grouped in front of the display, Misti read the card: "We'll miss you, Lew. The girls of Cheetah II."

"Isn't that sweet?" Misti whispered. "That's where I met Lew. Those girls were so nice to send this wreath." She signed. "I hope some of them show up so you can meet them. But they probably won't. You can't be a morning person in this business."

"Maybe this service is a little early," Andrea said. "I should have asked you about that when you planned it."

"That's OK. If it were later they would all be working. I like having this service now. Ten o'clock doesn't even seem early to me any more. My life has sure changed." She gently touched the dried pink roses. "This was my wedding bouquet. Lew bought it for me just before we went into the chapel in Vegas. It matched my dress, the one I am wearing today."

Jordan, who didn't often show her soft side, was beginning to cry. "That is the sweetest thing I've ever heard," she said, fishing in her bag for a tissue.

Half hidden behind the bouquet was a photo of Misti and Lew.

"It's kind of hard to see – that Elvis-looking guy behind Lew was our minister. A lady played *Love Me Tender* on a little organ and we all sang along – sort of like vows, you know? I used that picture of Lew for the notice in the paper. My Bunny Boy. It's the only photo I have of him." Misti seemed distracted, lost in happy memories.

"Not much of a looker, was he? I'm not into pale bald guys," Cay said under her breath to Jordan as they preceded the others to their seats.

"Shush," Jordan said. "She liked him. That's enough."

"You're right, Jordan. That's all that matters." Cay scooted over to accommodate Trish and Andrea in the pew. Misti continued to stand in front of the photo. The metallic threads in her pink spandex mini dress glittered in the morning sun coming through two tall windows.

The funeral attendant came forward carrying a brass urn, which he put on the table next to the dried wedding bouquet. Misti touched the urn. "Who would have dreamed my wedding dress would be my widow's weeds? It sounds like a country song." She gave the urn a little pat and then sat next to Andrea in the pew.

The soft sounds of an Elvis medley filtered into the room. *Viva Las Vegas* was followed by *Fools Rush In*, then *Heartbreak Hotel*.

"That was our story," Misty said wiping her eyes. "Elvis said it all."

The man in the dark suit returned and stood at the front of the room. "We are here today to memorialize Lew Cannon, to celebrate his life and mourn his death. Does anyone wish to say something about the departed?"

Misti raised her hand and took a piece of paper out of her purse. She walked a bit unsteadily to the front of the room and turned around.

As she unfolded a piece of paper, an agitated woman in full cry pulled everyone's attention to the back of the room. A sturdy brunette with glasses and an incongruously cheery embroidered sweater with red apples on the front charged into the chapel, waving the Atlanta paper.

"What the hell is going on here?" she demanded.

"Took the words right out of my mouth," Jordan said.

"Who is she?" Cay asked Andrea.

"Oh dear, I'm afraid I don't know."

"I want to know what a bunch of hookers are doing with my husband!"

A woman wearing a name tag labeled "grief counselor" hurried into the chapel and joined the director, who had been conducting the proceedings.

"Get away from me, you morons! I am Betty Pat Grimm, and you ran a picture of my husband Peter Grimm in the obituaries. It shows him right here," she said waving the paper, "and it says that you're having a memorial service for him here, right now. Only the name is for somebody else, and he isn't wearing his contacts and wig, which he always wore. I saw this over coffee this morning. Can you imagine? My husband, the father of our children, looking back at me from the obits."

Betty Pat was running out of breath. Trish felt it was up to her take charge. She stood up and walked toward Betty Pat, who was now only a few inches from Misti.

"Let's see if we can't figure this out calmly," Trish began.

"Calmly? Calmly?" Betty Pat's voice was ascending to glass-shattering heights. "How calm would you be if you found a bunch of hookers..."

"First of all, no one here is a hooker," Andrea stood beside Trish. "We are all respected members of the business community...."

"And what the hell business would that be? Who would wear that to a funeral?" Betty Pat pointed toward Misti's revealing hot pink dress.

"I wore it because it was my wedding dress," Misti folded her hands demurely and stared at Betty Pat. "Lew loved it."

"Who is this son-of-a-bitch Lew Cannon?" She thrusts the paper in Misti's face. "This picture is my husband. Unless he had a twin, and he did not, that is Peter Grimm and only Peter Grimm." She stopped and looked down at the brass urn.

"Jesus H. Christ! Is Peter in there? Did you burn him up and put him in there? The children didn't even get to say goodbye to their father." Betty Pat began to cry with gusto and Cay pushed some tissues in Andrea's hand to pass on.

"Oh, dear. I'm sure we can straighten out this unfortunate mix-up," the funeral director stammered.

"That is my poor Bunny Boy in there," Misti said, clutching the urn to her, "and nobody else."

"Bunny Boy? You called my husband Bunny Boy? I think I'm going to puke."

Instead of following through with the threat of nausea, Betty Pat grabbed for the urn and Misti clutched it more tightly.

"I'm betting on Misti," Cay said. "She is really strong. She's stronger than at least two men."

"But Betty Pat has craziness on her side," Jordan said. "You can't underestimate that."

Mother held up a bill. "I have a twenty says Misti can take her. Anybody want a piece of that?"

Isabelle hissed. "Mother, for God's sake, be quiet."

The two women continued to wrestle with the urn between them. Trish noticed the grief counselor was punching numbers into her cell phone. "That's a bad sign," she said to Jordan and Cay. "If she is calling for back-up, it might mean security, or it could mean the cops."

"I'm calling Bongiovanni," Jordan said.

"You have him on speed dial now?" Cay asked.

"I've always had him on speed dial," Jordan answered. "Since way back when."

"Oh, OK, just asking." Cay said.

Misti and Betty Pat hit the floor rolling around with the urn between them. The funeral director offered a few tentative "we can work this out" noises, but the women were locked in a deadly embrace and weren't letting go.

The telltale scratchy sound of a police radio didn't put a damper on the action. Two officers raced into the chapel guns drawn. Cay covered her ears and closed her eyes.

"No, no officers, I assure you…" Trish began.

"Stand back, lady, unless you want cuffs, too," one of the officers said. "OK, you two break it up or we're taking you both in."

"He means it," Jordan shouted. "Knock it off."

In an apparent moment of common sense, the two pulled apart. Betty Pat, with a firm hold on the lid of the urn and Misti still gripping the base, the ashes poured onto the wives and the carpet.

"Oh, yuck," Cay covered her eyes. "I can't look."

Dazed, both women were still while a policeman lectured them. Given the nature of the occasion, he decided not to take them in for disorderly conduct. No one moved as the police exited.

Betty Pat left screaming all the way up the aisle, "You haven't seen the last of me yet. I'm gonna get to the bottom of this mess and find out what's happened to my husband. You'll be hearing from my attorney."

"Oh, good," Cay said. "Just what we need, another crazy woman armed with an even crazier lawyer."

Jordan nudged Cay, "This whole scene is Lew all over the place. Get it?"

Cay glared.

"Well, now, this is much better," the director said. "Shall we continue with the service?"

"Shut up and get me the Hoover," Misti said. "I'm not leaving here without Lew."

Chapter 31

"Isabelle, will you have some good news for us when we get back?" Trish said into her cell. "When we left the Center this morning I got the impression you had been hard at work most of the night, deciphering the information on the key."

"I don't know if I'm looking forward to that or not," Misti said. "One shocker after another, bam. bam. bam. But I still love Lew." She patted the urn she held in her lap.

They rode in silence in the Justice Center van. When they arrived, Misti said, "Do you mind if I spend some time alone with Lew? You can check out Isabelle's findings now, if you want to, and I'll come down later. I need to sit with Lew and meditate. I learned that in yoga, you know, and it really calms me down. Centers me, as they say."

"That's fine, Misti," Andrea said. "You take a break. I think the rest of us are curious to see what Isabelle has found." Misti slowly climbed the stairs to her room, cradling Lew's urn, while the rest of the group went down the hall to the Center office. Isabelle still had the figures up on the computer screen.

"This is so interesting," Isabelle said, as if she were studying a newly discovered species. "It seems to be a highly condensed report of financial transactions from all over the world. Amounts paid, profits, trade routes, connections. There are even some drawings. Here," she scrolled down to a page of rough sketches. "Have any of you seen anything like this? Maybe Misti will recognize these."

"The Chix do, right?" Trish said, "Those drawings are the presses we found in the condo below Misti's. Does it say what they're for?"

"Not exactly, but here are some diagrams of how they work." Everyone leaned in closer to the screen. Isabelle pointed and continued. "I would say these presses were used to create something into shapes like the Styrofoam used to pack toaster ovens. See, doesn't this picture look sort of like that to you? You don't need the ovens. The packing materials are worth a whole lot, are light weight, and if they are noticed, they just look like trash."

Jordan said, "Brilliant. That is just brilliant. This is why the toaster ovens were at the dump. Ace must have smelled residual powder when we brought one into the Justice Center that night."

"Is there any clue as to who might have put this information together or why?" Cay asked.

Isabelle scrolled down the document. "I haven't found anything, but it is slow going, as I said. There appears to be a few names or maybe they are code names. The name 'Lapin' appears several times."

Trish squinted at the TV monitor, "Is M. Hozk listed anywhere?"

"No. That doesn't ring a bell, but it could well be in here. Proper names are hard to discern in Cyrillic. It could turn up. Why?" Isabelle said.

"Long story," Trish said to Isabelle. "Let's go back to 'Lapin.' My limited French tells me that Lapin means rabbit.

"As in Bunny Boy? Andrea asked.

"Quick thinking, Cuz," Trish smiled.

"I can think of someone else who might be the bunny," Cay said. "When we were in Misti's condo, I looked through one of her scrapbooks and there were pictures of her in a bunny costume. She was standing in front of a big neon sign, something about 'headlining' written on it, and there was another photo of her in bunny ears and not a lot more on a roof top. It looked like the Vegas strip was behind her. Remember, she got upset and snatched the book away from me."

"Every club in America must have had a bunny act at one time or another," Jordan said. "I wouldn't read too much into her scrapbooks."

"I think you all accept entirely too much from her as fact," Cay said. "I'm not accusing her of anything, but I think you ought to take the blinders off and start asking her some hard questions."

"What do you think this key might be for?" Trish asked. "Was someone trying to get this information to the FBI? Why would they entrust it to Misti or was it a chance encounter and she was at the wrong place at the wrong time? It raises more questions than it answers."

Isabelle adjusted her glasses. "Give me some time to finish reading the rest of this document before you make any firm decision about what to do with it. When you turn this over to Lanier or the proper authorities, you know they will freeze us out of any more information."

"I want to do some sleuthing closer to home," Jordan said. "I want to get up close and personal with Betty Pat who is now another possible suspect. Keep in mind that the original question was who killed Lew. It seems we ought to be following that trail first before we get carried away with the drug trade. We know the cops still suspect Misti of killing Lew. What we need to do is to point the finger at as an alternate real life suspect and get the spotlight off of Misti. Remember what Lanier said about 'reasonable doubt.' "

"Jordan, ever the practical one," Cay said.

"How about that sweater Betty Pat was wearing, the apple thing?" Jordan asked. "I think that hideous fashion statement alone makes her a candidate to be Lew's killer. She was a feisty little thing at the mortuary, and what if she knew her husband was a bigamist? I can definitely see her taking him out."

"Could Betty Pat get into the condo and wield a bowling ball? That early in the morning?" Andrea said.

"You think she needed coffee first?" Jordan asked.

"We don't know if Betty Pat knew about Misti," Trish said. "She may have thought everything was dandy with old Lew, or rather Peter Grimm. Maybe she was honestly shocked when she saw him in the obits with a different name and a different wife."

"She sure sounded shocked to me," Andrea said.

Jordan shook her head. "I don't know. Betty Pat would have had to ignore a lot, it seems to me. Of course the 'burbs' can do that to you. But we'll never figure it out sitting around here. There's just one thing to do."

"I recognize that look," Cay said. "Jordan, you are going to get us in trouble."

"Nonsense. We just have to find a good excuse to visit Betty Pat."

"I have the perfect reason to go see her," Trish said. "It's a Southern custom to take food to the family when someone dies. We'll get a roasted chicken – no, we'll get a whole dinner - for Betty Pat and the children, and we'll take it to her house and offer her our condolences."

"How do you know there are kids?" Cay asked.

"She screamed something about them at the memorial service," Trish said.

"Besides, why would you wear an apple sweater like that if you didn't have kids?" Jordan asked. "Stuff like that says, 'I'm a mother and I'm full of anger.' "

Cay winced. "What if she's full of anger at us? She saw us sitting with Misti at the memorial service. Maybe she'll call the cops if we show up on her front porch. Do we even know where Betty Pat lives?"

Jordan said, "I can find her address with my Blackberry. There's no reason not to get that chicken and go right now."

"Now?" Trish sounded a little alarmed. "I meant to cook dinner for her and the children. How can we go now?"

"We'll make one quick stop before we hit the Publix to buy the food." Jordan headed for the door, grabbing Trish by the arm.

"One stop? Where? Why?" Cay stammered.

"Just keep up, Cay. We're outta here." Jordan walked faster.

Chapter 32

"Why the hell am I doing this? Remind me." Cay sank further into the car seat. "Jordan, of all the crazy things you've made me do, visiting a psychic may be the most bizarre. I wish we had gone at night so no one could see us."

Trish turned around from the front seat of Jordan's van. "Cay, stop complaining. We are here to support Jordan in her quest to get some answers for her life. She doesn't want to leave any possible advice untapped. This will be just a short detour on our way to Publix and Betty Pat's."

"Couldn't we have just bought Jordan a Magic 8 Ball?" Cay whined.

"Listen you guys, one of my Jersey friends went to see a psychic in Spring Lake, and she foretold of a real estate venture. It totally came true, and my friend made a bundle. I'm so desperate for answers, I want to see what this woman has to say."

"So you think the great psychotic Madame Quintella of Roswell Road is going to give you a plan for the rest of your life?" Cay snorted, reading a brightly colored sign advertising Madame's psychic skills available just a few hundred yards away.

Jordan turned around, "Damn it, Cay, she's a PSYCHIC, not a psychotic, and I'd settle for a clue about the next couple of days."

"God, Jordan! Turn back around and look at the road. Otherwise none of us will have a next couple of days." Cay clutched her heart.

Trish pointed to the left. "There's her building, Jordan. There's parking in the rear. Tell me again where you heard about this woman?"

"I Googled her."

Cay raised her voice. "This is the final straw. I can't take it any more! Google? You chose a psychic from Google?"

Jordan turned so sharply into the parking lot, her tires squealed. "Well, she had the most hits, so she must be good. Right?"

"I'll stay in the car and take a nap. Wake me when it's over."

"Come on Cay, we are all in this together," said Trish in a no nonsense voice.

The Chix approached the crayon red front door of the blue house. They noticed the windows were painted black.

Cay brightened. "Love the Christmas lights. At least they're cheerful. What in the world have you talked me into Jordan? Is this woman into voodoo?"

Jordan glared and rang the doorbell and the tones of *Jingle Bells* could be heard from the inside of the house. The Chix exchanged a startled look. "That was unexpected," Trish said.

The woman who answered the door wore a bright floral print turban and a long flowing purple caftan. Hoop earrings dangled from her pierced ears and her arms were almost invisible beneath the multiple bracelets. "Come in. You are Jordan McKeehan, right?" She pointed at Jordan.

"Yeah, how did you know?"

"That's why you came. I know things."

Jordan smirked at Cay.

The Chix went into the living and dining room combination. They passed a plasma TV and comfortable chairs as they followed her into back room. The walls and ceiling were draped in black velvet. A paisley scarf covered a large round table with seating for eight in the center of the room.

Madame Quintella sniffed the air. "Apples. I smell apples. What do they mean to you?"

"Pie?" answered Cay hopefully.

"No, that's not it. Ah, well. Maybe it will be revealed during our session." She motioned the Chix into the chairs. "Let's proceed and maybe the answers you seek will become clearer."

Trish grabbed Cay's arm and positioned her on her right, with Jordan next. She nodded as Jordan linked her arm with Cay's.

Madame Quintella closed her eyes and told the ladies to do the same. Soft harp music began to play in the background. "Join hands. Everyone concentrate on the one thought that's most important to you," she said in a husky voice.

Cay peeked to make sure everyone else had their eyes closed.

"Close your eyes too, miss. You know who I'm talking to."

"We all know who you are talking to. Cay, cooperate!" Jordan let go of her hand and elbowed her.

"Romance. I see the aura of romance for all of you. That is highly irregular in a group reading. One of you still loves someone from college. There is trouble right now, but ultimately love will win out if you follow your heart. One has lost her love, but another will find you soon. He will be tall, fair, or maybe gray hair, and he will have the mantle of government on his shoulders.

"The third vision is a spiritual affair: unattainable, inappropriate, but a very powerful attraction. Be careful. You can't always judge a book by its cover."

"OK, I'm outta here. I'll be in the car." Cay jumped up, knocked over her chair, and fled the house.

"I'm sorry, but that's all for this session. The connection is broken for today. That will be one hundred and fifty dollars, please."

Jordan paid with her platinum American Express then she and Trish joined Cay in the car.

"Well, we know she hit a nerve with you, Cay. I don't get it, 'you can't judge a book by its cover'. Hmm, what does that mean? Could you protest too much? You blew up every time I said you were having a little something with one of those monks you work with, but maybe I was closer to home than you wanted." Jordan sighed. "I guess she's right about the college part, too. That is where I met Jimmy, but I'm still not sure if loving him is enough. He's got to love me back and commit to our marriage. What did you think of her, Trish?"

"I'm speechless. What she said was vague but some of it was accurate. I did "lose" my husband John to a heart attack, but another love? I'm not interested right now. What do you think the apple smell was all about? Have either of you been eating apples today?"

Cay sat up straighter. "No, but I'm all over going to McDonald's for their two for one fried apple pies. I know there is one by Publix farther up Roswell Road. Jordan, do you want to go through the drive-through or should we eat inside?"

Chapter 33

"I am glad we are eating inside," Trish said. "I hate drive-throughs. Makes the car smell like grease."

"So? I have a lot of good memories of grease," Jordan said. "Ah, the smell of fried onion rings in Jersey at Callahan's on 9W. Nothing like it."

As the Chix glanced at the menu Cay said, "It's comforting these places are always the same." She nudged Jordan. "Order. The cashier is waiting for you."

Jordan frowned as she turned to the bored looking teenager behind the counter. "I'll have a strawberry shake and large fries, please."

Trish asked, "How can you eat that and stay thin? There has to be some justice in the world. Maybe it will catch up with you one day." Trish smiled at the cashier. "I'll have a small salad, diet dressing, and double croutons."

Cay was next. "Ha! Miss Goody Two Shoes. There are probably as many calories in those croutons as in Jordan's fries. Give me the two fried pies and a small coffee."

"I'll jog an extra mile to burn the calories," Trish said.

Jordan picked up her order and sighed. "I feel better already. I knew I could count on you Cay."

They found a table and Cay started on her first fried pie, eyes closed in bliss.

Jordan shook her head. "So, the psychic wasn't to everyone's taste, was she?"

Cay said, "You know, this apple pie reminds me thing of something. The psychic said she smelled apples. Do you remember the memorial service for Lew when Betty Pat Grimm burst in? She had apples on her sweater, right?"

Trish nodded. "That whole episode was so tacky and awful, but maybe you have something. Think the psychic picked up on Betty Pat's outburst?"

Jordan wiped ketchup off her chin. "I kind of liked the memorial service. Sort of a Real Housewives of Atlanta moment. Well, we'll never figure it out sitting around here. Finish up and let's head north to Alpharetta and 'sleuth'. Oh, I just love the thought of that."

Cay said, " I recognize that look, Jordan. You are going to get us in trouble for sure."

"Nonsense." Jordan stood. "Thanks for Trish's genteel tradition of taking food to the bereaved family, we have the perfect excuse to visit the Grimm family. Toxic waste reclamation indeed. He has the perfect name for his occupation. Grimm Real Estate. Come on Chix. Let's find us some reasonable doubt."

Chapter 34

"This is very attractive. Nice plantings, quiet, everyone's yard in the neighborhood looks well cared for." Trish stood by the car and glanced around the cul de sac. "Peter Grimm seems to have provided nicely for Mrs. Grimm."

"Don't forget the little Grimmlins," Jordan rubbed her hands together. "I just like to say that. I can't help myself."

"Let's get on with this," Cay said. "I feel like I'm snooping."

"That's because you are snooping. I would have thought you picked up on that." Jordan tugged at her skirt. "Damn drycleaners. They shrink everything."

"Maybe those fries you eat have come back to haunt you and are making a little home on your thighs," Cay said. "Or maybe your skirt was a teensy bit too short to begin with. Just tossing out other possibilities. Get the food and let's get this over with. What should we look for?" Cay tucked her purse under the seat. One less thing to worry about if the Chix needed to make a quick getaway.

Trish responded, "Not sure. I guess the main thing is whether Betty Pat knew her husband was a bigamist before he was killed. If so, that could be her motive for murder. This could take some of the suspicion off Misti.

All we need is reasonable doubt, right? Be subtle, but find out if she has an alibi for the morning of Lew's murder."

"Got it. Now what should I look for?"

"Let's hope we know it when we see it, whatever 'it' is." Trish took the bag with the freshly baked chicken and Jordan picked up the vegetables. "Cay, get the rolls and cookies. All right, ready, Chix? Let's go."

They marched up to the front door and Cay, who was carrying the least, rang the bell. Jordan looked up at the apple flag flying from a front porch column and shook her head, "I don't get those flag things, but the subject matter is interesting, isn't it."

"Don't worry," Cay said. "You can't stick a flag out the window of a high rise at Twelve anyway. Do you think the psychic really was onto something? Beyond strange." Betty Pat opened the front door. She looked stunned.

"Mrs. Grimm, I'm Trish Townsend. This is Jordan McKeehan, and Cay Curtis. We wanted to express our condolences for your loss." Trish held out the chicken.

"Why...why isn't that sweet," Betty Pat relaxed a little and opened the door. "Please come in. Y'all look familiar. Don't I know y'all from somewhere?"

"We haven't really met. We attended the memorial service for your late husband."

"Of course! That's where I've seen you three. Listen, if you think..." She wiped her hands on an apple print dishtowel.

"We don't think anything," Cay said nudging Trish to the side. "Nothing at all. We didn't even know the deceased. We are friends of Andrea Simmons, and she created the Women's Justice Center...and..."

"And we were just lending her our moral support." Trish finished Cay's sentence. "Mrs. Grimm, we would like to make amends for any unhappiness you experienced so we brought you and your children a little something for dinner." Trish brushed by Betty Pat as she entered into the front hall.

Betty Pat was completely confused. "Well, thank you, I guess. Why don't you put the food in the kitchen?"

"I can do that," Cay said. "Jordan, you help me unpack everything. Mrs. Grimm, you just relax and talk to Trish. She's Southern too, you know. Why did I say that? Oh, well, come on Jordan."

"Please call me Betty Pat," she said as Trish took her arm and led her into the living room.

"Why don't we sit down over here?" Trish maneuvered Betty Pat away from the kitchen door onto a sofa in the far corner so Jordan and Cay could snoop unobserved.

Cay grabbed the bag with the chicken and hurried to the kitchen with Jordan. Whispering, she nodded toward a built-in desk, "Hey. This looks like an office center. A computer, files, even family mail. Keep an eye out. I'm going to look through some of this stuff."

"Cay, you sound like an old pro. I'm beginning to have a good influence on you. I'm so proud." Jordan took up her watch near the door. "We should try to look in the medicine cabinet in the master bathroom. How do you think we arrange that?"

"We could ask for a house tour, and then when we get up there I could have a sudden urge. I'm pretty good with bathrooms, if you'll remember. Back when Andrea was accused of Sonny's murder, I found out all kinds of interesting stuff when I used the bathroom in that dumpy little Global Industries or whatever it was. I'd say I was just about the queen of bathroom sleuthing." Cay was pulling out files, reading the labels and putting them back.

"And it's a title you are welcome to, hon. I'll give you no competition there. Wait a minute. She's coming!" Jordan jumped back from the door. When she turned around, Cay was calmly rearranging a few things in the refrigerator to make room for the chicken.

"I was wondering what happened to you girls. Everything OK?" Betty Pat glanced at her watch.

"Hunky dory," Jordan said. "We will be right there. We didn't want to squash the, er, squash."

"I have to pick the children up at school pretty soon. Not that I am hurrying you. It's just that carpool can be such a mess."

"Of course. Hurry it up, girls," Trish said following Betty Pat into the kitchen. "Just one more thing, Betty Pat. Could you identify some of your family in your photographs on your mantle? I just love family portraits. Genealogy is a passion of mine." She redirected Betty Pat back to the living room.

As soon as Betty Pat was distracted, Jordan said, "Get going, Cay. This may be our only chance. I'll put the rest of the food away. You look for something – anything."

"Maybe this is what we want," Cay said. "It's in the file for credit card bills. Thank God the woman is organized. It looks like Peter Grimm's credit card statements. The one on the top is for the period ending ...let's see..."

"OK, OK. What does it say?" Jordan asked.

"Well, it has two plane tickets to Vegas charged on it, and let's see. Yep, and here are charges for the wedding chapel. I'll bet Betty Pat found that extremely interesting. The question is, did she find it before or after he was murdered?"

"We can figure that out later. Just take it."

"Take it? Won't she suspect us? Jordan, we've spent ages in this kitchen alone and she knows we had some connection to her husband because we were at the memorial service. It doesn't matter what kind of spin Trish puts on it."

Jordan snatched the statement from Cay's hand and stuck it inside her bra. "There. Done. We're outta here."

"All finished," Jordan called out cheerily as they returned to the living room. "Sorry we took so long, I wanted things to be organized. Nice apple theme by the way. Well, time flies. I guess we should be going." She motioned to Trish to stand up.

"I guess we should," Trish said. "You take care of yourself, Betty Pat. Bless your heart, you have had quite a shock. I can tell that you are one of those people who just gives, gives, gives. Please make some time for yourself."

Jordan and Cay were already out the door. Trish hurried to catch up. "Good heavens. Could you leave any faster? What did you find?"

"Jump in the car and we'll tell you on the way home." Jordan started the van.

"That place was just plain strange," Cay said. "Everything there was apples."

"Oh. I didn't notice," Jordan said.

"It's a daddy thing," Trish said. "When we were looking at her needlepoint apple pillows she told me her father was known as the 'Apple King of Ellijay.'"

"Then even stranger," Cay said. "And I didn't even get to sleuth in the bathroom."

"Here," Jordan said, reaching inside her bra and pulling out the credit card statement. "Check this out. You can be sure Peter Grimm didn't intend for Betty Pat to see this."

Trish looked at the statement. "The closing date was before Peter or Lew or whoever he was got killed. I guess the question is, when did Betty Pat see it? BB or AB?"

"BB? Oh, Before Bowling Ball. Then it should be BBB," Cay said. "You know, we probably don't even have to find the answer to that. Isn't the fact that she had that statement enough to cast doubt on Misti's guilt? We don't have to pin the crime on someone else. We just have to show that there was someone besides Misti with means, motive, and opportunity. Am I right?"

"Always. Now what should we do with this evidence?" Jordan asked. "Give it to Lanier? Or if I have to, I could call Jerry."

"Let's take it to Lanier first," Trish said. "Jordan you do it. I took him that toaster from the dump and then returned with the empty box. I am a little embarrassed to tell him we stole this too."

"He's used to criminals," Jordan said. "He'll be cool with it."

Trish nodded. "I'll take that as a yes."

"On the way home, can we go through MacDonald's and get another fried apple pie?" Cay asked. "I am getting a real yen for another one. They help calm me down. One woman's Valium is another woman's fried pie. You can quote me on that." Cay leaned back in her seat and closed her eyes. "Who would have thought belonging to a book club could be so stressful?"

Less than an hour after the Chix pulled into the MacDonald's a plain white Crown Victoria sedan pulled into the far right lane going toward Betty Pat's exit on Georgia 400.

Chapter 35

Jerry turned right into Betty Pat's subdivision. "I don't get it. Every damn street has the same name." Detective Bongiovanni was peering at the street signs in the Alpharetta subdivision.

"No, not exactly the same, Jerry," Helen Morrow replied. "See, this is Meadow Grove Way. The next street we cross is Meadow Grove Court, and then we turn right onto Meadow Grove Chase. The Grimm house is at the end of this cul de sac. Looks like you can park right in front."

"That's another damn thing," Jerry said. "Half of these streets are dead ends. More than half. You could be trapped in here for days – weeks."

"They aren't dead ends. They are cul de sacs. You know that. You are just being difficult because you don't like the 'burbs and you had to drive for once. I always drive and you do your paperwork. Then I'm stuck back at the station finishing my work while you breeze on out. Not this time, Buster."

"When was the last time I 'breezed on out,' as you put it? I put in more hours than anybody. Don't tell me. The house with that stupid apple flag in the front, right?" Jerry eased the Crown Vic to the curb. "Apples? What the hell?"

"Wholesome, I guess," Helen said. "That sort of thing is popular in neighborhoods like this."

They looked around as they walked toward the front door.

"Sure is quiet," Jerry said. "You'd think that this time of day kids would be home from school and at least a few of them would be outside. Street hockey, stuff like that."

"Street hockey? Jerry, where have you been? Any kids who are playing hockey are in arenas, wearing pro-style uniforms, coached by crazed adults. They don't do 'pick-up' out here."

"Their loss," Jerry said, ringing the doorbell. A wreath on the door was trimmed with wooden apples.

"Hot for apples, isn't she? What's up with that, do you think?" Jerry asked.

"Jerry, sometimes an apple is just an apple, you know what I mean? Don't overwork it." Helen rang the bell again.

Betty Pat Grimm opened the door. She was wearing a tense smile and an apron over her sweater and denim skirt. The apron's pockets were large red gingham apples.

Helen flashed her badge. "Mrs. Grimm? I'm Atlanta Police Detective Morrow and this is my partner Detective Bongiovanni. We need to ask you some questions about your husband, Peter Grimm."

"Come in, please. I've been expecting you. Excuse the mess. We just got home from school." A Golden Retriever shot past them and into the kitchen, disappearing around a corner.

"Delicious! Rowdy dog. Macintosh, get Delicious and put him outside," she said to a girl who appeared next to her, silent and frowning. "Do it now. Honestly, I have to do everything myself." The detectives followed Betty Pat into the kitchen. "I am cooking for the Presidents' Day bake sale at the children's school. This is such a busy time, but I do want to answer your questions. Just a minute, let me shoo my children out of the kitchen. They don't need to hear us, poor things." She wiped her hands on her apron. Bongiovanni glanced at the spotless floor.

"Who's that?" A boy sitting at the kitchen table asked, eyeing Bongiovanni from beneath dark bangs.

"Just some people taking a survey, dear. Take your sister and go in the den. You can play a video game. Special treat." When neither child moved, Betty Pat upped the stakes. "Macintosh! Fuji! March or it's no desert for you tonight."

When the two had left the room she said in a conspiratorial voice, "It's their favorite – apple pie."

"Who would have ever guessed?" Helen said.

"You probably think I've gone overboard for apples, don't you? My daddy was the Apple King of Ellijay. Funny. I just told that to three women who were here earlier. They were at Peter's memorial service with that damned hooker." Helen and Jerry exchanged glances.

Bongiovanni gritted his teeth. "Was one a tall, well dressed blond, another wearing Birkenstocks and tortoise shell glasses and a third with red curls?"

"Yes, how did you know?" Betty Pat looked puzzled.

"Just a lucky guess. Go on with your story, Mrs. Grimm." Jerry took out his note pad.

"Alright. I probably haven't mentioned it in years but that's what he was called: The Apple King. I grew up loving everything about apples – still do. Oh, Daddy didn't want me to marry Peter. He said I could do so much better, but I wouldn't listen. We were happy, at least for a long time. No kids came along so we adopted. We went to Korea and got Fuji…"

Helen interrupted. "Excuse me, but isn't that a Japanese name? Like Mount Fuji?"

"It doesn't matter. It's all sort of the same over there, all so foreign. You know what I mean? As soon as we got settled at home, I was pregnant with Macintosh." Betty Pat took a tissue out of her apron pocket and dabbed her eyes. "Listen to me running on. None of this probably matters to you, does it? Could I get you a cup of coffee or a co'cola or some iced tea?"

"No thank you, Mrs. Grimm. We have some questions about your husband," Bongiovanni said in a gentle voice. Helen looked at him, surprised by his tone, which was usually gruff.

"I can't be much help there, I'm afraid," Betty Pat said. "Peter bought and sold real estate. Sometimes he bought places that were toxic, you know? Needed clean-up, EPA kind of stuff. When he got them approved, he'd turn around and sell them. He was all over the place – Florida, South Carolina, Alabama. He was usually gone for days at a time, a week even. But he was always glad to see me when he got home, and of course he was crazy about the kids.

"This is such a horrible, horrible shock. Murdered and supposedly married to that trashy pole dancer." She took another tissue out of her pocket and blew her nose. "I can't imagine what got into him."

"Did you ever meet any of the people your husband worked with?" Helen asked.

Betty Pat shook her head. "Peter was not much for socializing. I don't know who he worked with. He never talked about his work. He said he needed to get away from all that filth when he came home. 'Filth' is exactly what he called it."

"Do you think he had enemies?" Helen looked up from her note pad. "Anyone who would want to hurt him?"

"Peter was a very gentle man. I can't imagine some-one would hate him enough to…to…." Betty Pat began to cry, holding an apple-print dishtowel to her eyes.

"I know this is painful," Bongiovanni said, "but we need to talk about the day he was killed. Do you recall what you were doing that day?"

"Me? You don't think I could have anything to do with my husband's murder do you?"

"This is a routine question, Mrs. Grimm. We have to explore all the possibilities." Jerry spoke softly. "I know this is upsetting, but we do need your help in finding his murderer."

"Would anything help you remember?" Helen offered. "A calendar, or..."

"Oh, I know exactly where I was the day Peter was murdered. I was attending the Girl Scout Council of the Northern District of Georgia. I am a leader, you know, and very involved in several statewide planning committees. We were having our annual breakfast kickoff meeting at the World Congress Center in downtown Atlanta, followed by a full day of workshops and conferences. There must have been at least several hundred people who heard me give a report – maybe more. It began very early, and I was there all I was there all day."

A few more questions and Bongiovanni wrapped it up, handing Betty Pat Grimm his card. "If you think of anything else, no matter how small, give me a call. All right?"

Betty Pat nodded and opened the front door. She looked at the conspicuous Crown Vic at the curb. Now the whole neighborhood – whole subdivision - would be gossiping. It was bad enough her husband was killed but the way it happened was just plain tacky. What was he thinking? Maybe she should move.

Bongiovanni tried to toss the keys to Morrow, but she batted them back."Oh no, you don't. Round trip. I'll work on the report."

As they pulled into the street, Bongiovanni hit his hand on the steering wheel. "How come the LitChix are always a step ahead of us? How many times do I have to tell them to keep their noses out of police business. They are going to talk to the wrong person someday and become victims themselves."

Helen nodded. "They're nothing but trouble, I've told you that more than once. Damn snoops."

Biogiovanni sighed deeply. "Getting back to Betty Pat, do you think she's a suspect?"

"If you mean am I convinced she couldn't have done it because of the Girl Scout thing, my answer is no. It wouldn't take long to get from the World Congress Center to the Marietta Street condo. and that was a conveniently early meeting. Did anyone tell her he was murdered around seven or seven –thirty a.m.? It is possible Betty Pat did an early meet and greet at the World Congress Center or even gave her speech, then slipped out, whacked him, and returned to the meeting. With a crowd that size no one would have noticed."

"So, back to my question: do you think she is a suspect?"

"Honestly?" Helen hesitated, then sat up straighter. "No, I don't. For one thing, what time was that explosion at the yoga studio? Seven fifteen, seven twenty at the latest? When did Misti get there? Probably around seven thirty. She would have been back home by seven forty-five. No way Betty Pat could have gotten in and out of their condo that fast. Why would she kill the bastard anyway? Because she found out he was a bigamist? Because she thought she had something to gain financially? Something about his work that was a real serious turn-off? Nope. No way she could have gotten there, killed him, cleaned up the apartment – don't forget it was as clean as a hospital in there - and gotten out in that fifteen minute window. Misti is still at the top of my list of suspects."

Helen looked out the car window. "Actually I feel sorry for Betty Pat. Losing her husband in such a public and horrific way. With all the media attention, she is bound to be humiliated. What could she possibly tell her kids about how their father died?"

"Getting soft, Morrow?" Bongiovanni asked. "The other day you were as hard as nails. No cruel indictment for Betty Pat? That mood passed?"

"No, not exactly. The other day I was just so damn angry, but I can't stay that way. Eats me up." She squirmed and crossed her legs.

"Want to share?

"Not really." Morrow said. "Leave the personal stuff at home, I always say, and then I do just the opposite." She shook her head. "I'm good."

"Yeah, right," Jerry answered.

"What's that supposed to mean?"

"Aren't you afraid of getting old and bitter and suspicious of everybody?" Jerry asked. "Sucked dry by the job?"

"Well on that cheerful note…"

"I mean it," he continued. "Sometimes I think about quitting."

"You aren't going to quit, Jerry. You're a cop through and through. You wouldn't know what to do if you weren't on the force."

"Would you?" Jerry asked. "We're a lot alike."

"Yeah," Morrow grinned ruefully. "That's what scares me."

Chapter 36

The polished Queen Anne dining room table, a hold-over from Andrea's former residence reflected the early morning sun. Bowls of mixed fruit and an assortment of muffins were on the table. So far, Andrea was the only one seated and she was studying a legal pad filled with notes. She looked up as the front door opened. Trish called out, "Yoo hoo! Anybody home?"

"In here, Trish," Andrea smiled. "Hi, Cuz. At least you and I are here. No sign of Jordan or Cay. Mother and Isabelle will join us when everyone else gets here."

Trish sat across the table. "I am exhausted. I need more sleep. All this tension and sleuthing to exonerate Misti is keeping me from feeling rested." She ladled some berries onto a Tiffany china plate. "What is on the agenda today?"

"I'd like to wait until we are all here, "Andrea said. "No reason to repeat myself."

"Makes sense," Trish said, noting the seriousness in Andrea's voice. They ate silently for a few more minutes until Jordan arrived, wearing large sunglasses and a Yankee baseball cap.

"You look like an unmade bed," Andrea said. "Are you all right?"

"Just a tad hung over," she said. "I need coffee".

"It's right there on the side board," Andrea said. "Help yourself."

Jordan skipped the china cups and went into the kitchen. She came back with an oversized mug. "I need a lot of coffee."

As she sat down, Cay arrived. "Good Morning," she thrilled. "What's up?"

"How can you be so damn cheery this time of the morning?" Jordan asked. "Did you get laid last night or something?"

"Or something," Cay replied and poured a cup of coffee. She sat down still smiling. "Oh, my what yummy looking muffins. Blueberry and apple cinnamon. Good choices. Andrea. Jordan, are you suffering mentally or physically this morning?"

Jordan glared and drank her coffee.

Andrea stood. "I'll call Isabelle and Mother on the intercom. Part of this meeting has to do with them."

"No Misti?" Jordan asked.

"Not today. This is just for the employees and active board members of the Justice Center, so as soon as they arrive, we'll start the meeting."

When Mother and Isabelle were seated, Andrea began. "Ladies, we have two important issues. One is the possible evidence that you have accumulated for Misti's defense. The second item is the Justice Center Open House this week." Andrea studied her legal pad. "First, we should talk about the evidence.

"Chix, as you know, I am eternally grateful for your sleuthing to find exonerating facts to help the unjustly accused. You certainly saved me when I was accused of my Sonny's murder, and I know you want to do as much for Misti."

"I feel a 'however' coming on," Cay said.

"However, all this information needs to be turned over to Lanier Poole or to the police as soon as possible. In the worst case scenario, our Board members could be accused of obstructing justice, interfering with prosecution, even conspiracy, for heaven's sake. While it would be awful for each of you individually, it would sink the Justice Center. It is enough of a challenge to start a facility that offers help to those who need it. Frankly, our clientele would not be popular in any neighborhood, period. If we are less than squeaky clean, well, I know you understand. Therefore..."

Cay said, "Could've predicted that 'therefore.'" She picked up another muffin.

"As I was saying, therefore, you need to, call Jerry or Lanier or both. Today. Get these clues or whatever they are disposed of to the proper authorities. Let's get this issue lifted now. Understood?" The Chix nodded. "Good. Moving on to the Open House. Isabelle, do you want to tell us what we can do to help you and Mother with that event?"

"Yes, thank you, Andrea," Isabelle replied. "Taking Andrea's instructions to heart, Mother and I have been arranging the Grand Opening party for our board, major donors, city and state elected officials and our Grant Park neighbors. People can visit with us, tour the Center, and take home a lovely brochure. It will have something about the history of the building when it opened as a church in the late 1880's, some before and after photographs, current floor plans, our mission statement, our operating staff and board members, and plans for the future." Isabelle handed around a glossy full-color tri-fold brochure worthy of a corporate empire.

"Who did this?" Trish asked. "It's professional and looks expensive."

Mother raised her hand. "I did, girls. I love photography and we purchased a sweet little digital camera. We also have a very efficient top quality printer, in case you don't know. The cost of the glossy paper and ink are the only expenses." Mother beamed. "I'm glad you like them. I may be an 'old' dog, but I have acquired a few new tricks."

"I'm impressed," Jordan said. "These are really classy."

"Since Misti is our only resident, who are the locals are supposed to meet?" Cay asked.

"Good point," Andrea answered. "Just us, the rest of the board and some of our major donors. Honestly, I think it would be condescending to put residents on parade."

"And risky," Cay said.

"Will we have more residents by the Open House?" Trish asked.

"Maybe, but probably not," Andrea answered. "I want to start slowly and be cautious with who we accept."

"Just like we were with Misti," Cay said.

"Misti was an exceptional situation," Andrea said. "In the morning I will start meeting with a couple of local agencies who will be making referrals to us. After that we should have an increase in residents. I am sure that there are more women out there who need the Center than we can take. I did ask a couple of other people in addition to media representatives.

"One of our U.S. Senators, Clayton Calhoun, is a close friend of Lanier's and having his support will be very good for us. Jack Cannon, the young attorney who will be our staff counsel is included, of course Lanier has been wonderful, but we can't expect him to donate his time forever. Besides we need an attorney familiar with poverty law and government aid programs. Jack will be available full time and will conduct legal rights classes, represent our clients, and be 'of counsel' to the Justice Center."

"Is he married?" Jordan asked.

"I don't know," Andrea frowned, "and that was not a condition of employment. Please, let's keep this business-like. I don't want us to be hit with a sexual harassment suit by our own lawyer."

"I thought if he were young, good looking and poor, he might be just the kind of man you're looking for." Jordan said.

"I'm not looking, and certainly not this close to home. Can we finish up here?" Andrea shuffled her pages. "The Junior League of Atlanta will be scheduling volunteers for sorting donations of clothing, books and furniture. They are making us one of their placements. Also, the Georgia Aquarium will host our first major fund raiser in the fall."

"Amazing, Andrea," Trish said. "You've done some very creative and worthwhile planning."

Andrea nodded and grinned. "Ok, we have less than a week to get ready for the Open House, so let's get moving. Mother has a list of chores and schedules posted on the kitchen bulletin board. After you Chix call Lanier or Jerry, you can check in with Mother and see how else you can help. I think that's all for now. Any other business or questions?"

"I have to go to work," Cay said. "I'll leave the calling and confessing to Trish and Jordan. I didn't see a thing. That applies to any question that might be directed my way. See you guys later." She took her keys to her old Volvo wagon out of her purse and left.

"She certainly seemed cheery today, didn't she?" Jordan said.

"She likes her work," Trish said.

"I think there's more to her good mood than work. Cay is so private, but I'm just the gal to get to the bottom of this mystery." Jordan stood. "Right now, can I call Jerry and throw myself on him for mercy?"

"That question alone makes me say absolutely not," Trish said. "I'll call Lanier first to determine the legality of what we have found. We can start with something concrete, like the condo keys we found in the hidden drawer in Lew's desk. Lanier will probably turn them over to the police, but I feel safer this way. I am not sure how to approach the subject of Peter Grimm's credit card statement."

"What about the USB key?" Jordan asked. "That seems extremely important especially since Mother was almost killed over it. Hey, the mob might send someone else over here if they think we still have it."

"Good point. Let's get Lanier's advice on how to handle the USB key first thing," Trish said.

"I have just a bit more work to do before we lose control of the information," Isabelle said. "I think I made a breakthrough understanding one last part that has been giving me fits. If I can have just a teensy bit more time, perhaps we will have some solid support for Misti's innocence."

"I'd just like to get that damn key out of here. It's caused us enough grief and trouble." Jordan said.

"Me too," Andrea said.

"We'll get it out of here soon, I promise," Trish said. "By the way, where is Misti? Sleeping in?"

"No, she just said she had errands and wanted to get started early."

"Well, Trish, I am sure you can handle all this without me. I am going to Twelve. I cannot wait to move in there but first I need to do some measuring. Today might be the day I have my own place!"

"It won't happen that fast, Jordan, I promise you."

"You never know how fast you can make a deal when it's for cash," she said.

Andrea frowned. "Are you kidding me? Cash? You would actually pay over three hundred thousand dollars in cash? Jordan, that is just not wise. You and Jim are not legally separated. Aren't you moving too fast? Besides, your parents left you money for your security, not to throw it away on a wild idea."

"A killer condo of my own is not a wild idea. When is real estate ever a bad investment? It's better than money in the bank." Jordan grabbed her purse and hurried out.

Chapter 37

"You're sure I can go to church dressed like this?" Misti pulled her purple mini-skirt as low as she could.

"Of course." Andrea said. "The Buckhead Church is very informal and isn't like any other church you have ever attended,"

"Not a contest since I haven't been to church since I was thirteen. I never imagined you wouldn't have to look proper, you know, to impress other people. I thought one of the main reasons people went was to see what everyone else was wearing."

Andrea pulled the Justice Center van into the Piedmont Road Starbucks parking lot across from The Buckhead Church. She spotted Trish's dark green Land Rover and rolled down her window. "Jump in Cuz. Who's that with you? Oh, Coleman! It's great to see you again. Trish told me you might come to Atlanta for a visit, but she wasn't sure when."

"Hey everybody," Trish said, as she climbed into the front seat. "Misti! I am so glad you decided to come with us today." She turned to face the rear of the van as Coleman took a seat in the middle. "Misti, this is my cousin, Coleman Butler. He is visiting from Lake City, Florida. Andrea and I grew up with him."

Looking back to the third row, to the collection of teenagers accompanying them, Trish spoke louder, "Kids, y'all remember Uncle Coleman, don't you?" There was a collective grunt of acknowledgment.

Coleman dressed as if he were going to a Tom Wolfe look alike party in his three piece cream colored seersucker suit. His Oliver Peoples wire-framed glasses were perched low on his pale patrician nose. "Hi kids. It's good to see y'all." He gestured in their direction with his ivory-handled cane.

"What brings you to town, Coleman?" Andrea asked.

"Why, Darling, this is a great time of year for Atlanta arts, and it is so pretty in the spring, I just had to come. I am quite an avid gardener, you know, so seeing these great old plantings of azaleas and dogwoods, blooming together, well it just takes my breath away. This week is the last of the opera season and there is a new exhibit at the High Museum. I sound like the Chamber of Commerce, don't I. I have a full agenda of things to do and see." He gave a little giggle.

"I think you should come to the Justice Center Open House," Andrea said. "It would show you what Trish and I been accomplishing these last months."

"Why, I would dearly love to. You know my mother loves to give to good causes. Maybe we can pry a little money out of her hands. She can't take it with her," he said, and giggled again. "Will this fetching creature be there?" he asked gawking at Misti.

Misti said, "Oh, well I don't really..."

"Of course she will," Andrea said. "Won't you, Misti? It will help with our fundraising."

"I guess so," Misti said.

"Then I absolutely would not miss it," Coleman said, his cheeks as pink as his bowtie.

***

"Cay, I want company," Jordan said talking into her cell. "Can you meet me at Twelve? It'll be a quick visit. I want to take some measurements of the new condo Trish found for me to use to draw a floor plan. What? No, I am not going to 'wing it'. I want to know exactly where to place my new furniture and what colors to paint the walls. I need your good eye for advice. Thanks. You are a good pal. I'll buy you lunch." She hung up and muttered, "Food. It gets her every time."

An hour later, Jordan and Cay were standing in her condo. "Did you really buy this?" Cay asked.

"Yes, I did, and please don't spoil it by saying anything negative. That's why I wanted you to come with me instead of Trish. She just won't let me enjoy it for a minute. She is so hung up about Jim and me, and besides she wanted me to go to The Buckhead Church with her this morning. This is my church, right here, at Twelve." Jordan sighed and twirled around.

"She mentioned it to me, too," Cay said. "That rock/pop thing isn't for me. I like some chanting, a little incense, and Latin is always good."

"Do you know how good it feels to have my very own key to my very own home? I don't have to share this with anyone if I don't want to. Trish thought it cost too much, but I think it's priceless. I can hardly wait to paint and furnish it. Here, hold one end of this tape."

"Does this mean you are divorcing Jim?" Cay asked as she held the tape for Jordan.

"I'm not sure," Jordan replied. "Now I feel as if I have time to think and evaluate my choices, because I have my retreat. If all women had their own apartments there would be fewer divorces. Cay, what the hell are you doing?"

Cay squinted out the balcony window. "I think I can see The Flying Biscuit on Tenth Street from here. I can taste the cheese grits now. They say they're famous for their biscuits, but those grits are the star in my book. They use cream cheese, you know. Cream cheese is the secret for great grits."

Jordan sighed. "Damn it, Cay. Pick up that tape. I like decorating and you like food. I did promise lunch, but not until we finish here first. Work to earn your treat."

Chapter 38

Exiting the church with a swarm of enthusiastic worshippers, Trish asked, "How did you like the service, Coleman?"

"What? Oh it was quite different. Not like any church I've ever attended before." he said, keeping his gaze fixed on Misti. "Would you permit me to ask you to dinner sometime?" he asked Misti. "Maybe a theatrical performance?"

"I don't do that any more. Oh, are you asking me for a date?" Misti couldn't hide her astonishment. "Yeah, sure, I guess so. I'm in mourning for my late husband, Lew, but a little fun couldn't hurt. He would want me to get on with life. Gum?" The scent of Juicy Fruit filled the air.

* * *

Cay dropped a bag of biscuits on the Justice Center office desk.

Jordan said, "We got a call from Trish to meet her here. Cay and I thought you and Mother might like something from The Flying Biscuit."

Isabelle looked up from the computer. "Thank you, that's very thoughtful. Oh, Jordan, you have a telephone message. Detective Bongiovanni would like for you to call him." Isabelle handed Jordan the carefully written message. "On Sunday. Does that man ever take a day off?"

Jordan grinned and snatched the paper. Cay said, "Trish said she heard something from Lanier. Do you know anything about that?"

"No, at least he didn't call here."

"I wonder why everyone is so busy all of a sudden" Cay said. "We don't hear a word and suddenly, when I could be reading the Sunday Times everyone wants a piece of me." She reached into the bag and took a bite of biscuit.

Jordan stepped into the hallway and snapped open her cell. "So Jerry, I got your message to call. Uh huh...uh huh. Well, sure...We'll be here...'Bye." Jordan slowly hung up. "He wasn't in a very chatty mood. He's heading over here now. Do I look OK?" Jordan hurriedly applied more chapstick. "Is Misti back yet? He wants her to hear what he has to say, too."

"Who wants me to hear what?" Misti asked, coming into the room.

"Detective Bongiovanni. He says he needs to talk to all of us," Jordan said.

"Do I need to say in my church clothes, or can I get comfortable?" Misti asked.

"Get comfortable, by all means," Cay said. After Misti left, she said, "Goodness knows, could it be possible to wear even less than she wore to church?"

Jordan yelled, "Trish, Andrea, Mother, join us in the living room. Bongiovanni is on the way and wants to talk to all of us."

Mother wheeled in the tea cart. "I love this thing," she said. "So handy and hospitable. Do you think the Detective would like some buttermilk pie?"

"Probably not," Cay said, "but I would. Thank you, Mother. This looks really good." Cay took a plate and cut a piece of the pie.

"Just coffee for me," Jordan said, pouring herself a mug half full and adding her usual six Splendas. "Too much coffee spoils the whole thing," she said, filling the rest of her cup with half and half. "Oh boy, there's the doorbell," Jordan spilled some of the cream. "Why am I so nervous?"

Andrea opened the door. Bongiovanni came in, but without the usual pleasantries. Andrea showed him to the living room where everyone but Misti was waiting.

Trish stood and smiled. "Hi, Jerry. Would you like some coffee and a piece of pie?"

"Not today, thanks. Would one of you please call Misti?" he asked. "I think this is information everyone needs to hear."

Misti came downstairs wearing cut-offs and a halter top. "What's going on?" she asked.

Cay whispered, "If I wanted to see navels I would go to the beach. Brother."

Jerry started pacing. "Some keys were delivered to the APD from Lanier Poole's office. They are considered to be part of the ongoing investigation of Lew Cannon's murder. Those keys had been in a secret drawer in the Cannon apartment until one of you Chix found them. The accompanying statement said," and here Bongiovanni read from his note pad, "the three of you and Misti used one of those keys to enter the unit directly below the Cannon's. There you found empty toaster oven boxes, equipment that appeared to be some form of die press, and white powder. When we took the key and went to the apartment to verify that statement, the condo was empty."

Trish jumped up. "How is that be possible? There was a lot of heavy looking equipment in there."

"I don't know what you all saw, but the condo is empty now. Just as in the Cannon condo, that unit has been washed down with bleach." Jerry pointed angrily at the Chix. "If you ladies would stop trying to do my job and maybe give me, oh, a little heads up when you snoop; then, maybe, just, maybe, the police could have seen the evidence for ourselves. But no, you took matters into your own hands and left the Atlanta Police Department out of the loop."

"So there's no more evidence?" Misti asked.

"I didn't say that." Jerry said running his fingers through his hair. "Fortunately, one of the properties of cocaine and other powder drugs is they are sticky and will cling to anything. Whoever cleaned the apartment forgot one thing. They didn't thoroughly clean the fluorescent lights. These little suckers give up the evidence every time."

"Get to the point, Jerry. What does all of this mean?" Jordan was getting annoyed with his demeanor.

"What it means is this. The owner of that condo is screwed. It's just a step from the presence of drugs, to evidence of a drug lab, to Lew and Lew's murderer. Fingerprints and trace evidence would have helped a lot. "

"And you want us to ask, don't you, who is the owner of that condo?" Jordan said.

"Ownership wasn't so easy to find, but we have research people who do some excellent work, and it seems that the primary owner, well protected by a corporate veil, but not well enough, is Mrs. Lew Cannon. Congratulations, Misti. You are left holding the bag."

"You're here to arrest me? You can't do that," Misti said.

"Well, actually, I can, but no, I am not here to arrest you. This is a courtesy call. Do not leave the jurisdiction. I can guaran-Goddamn-tee you murder and drug trafficking charges are in your near future. Now, while you all mull this over, I would like to speak to Jordan in private."

"I don't know if I am in the mood to speak to you," Jordan said. "Where do get off on this Law and Order macho cop routine?"

"Take it to the library," Andrea said. "We have things to discuss out here."

Jordan closed the library door behind them. "I don't mind telling you I'm pissed, Jerry. You come in here, Mr. Police Procedure. We were the ones that gave the police the condo key, and we were the ones that tipped you about the contents of that condo, and then you have the gall to come over here and tell us Misti is about to be arrested? That's crazy. Why would she have gone with us through this whole thing if she was a criminal? Why would she let us go into her condo to search for evidence of her innocence? 'Oh here, you found the keys, and hey, let's look inside that condo, and wow, there's drug stuff inside and oops, guess I'm caught.' I don't think so, you big dope."

Jordan jabbed Jerry's chest with her finger. "Lew could have put his condo in Misti's name to keep that looney Betty Pat from getting it. In fact, he could have put tons of stuff in Misti's name. Who's to say Misti knew? She knew about the condo they lived in, period, and she told you about that."

They were still standing just inside the library door. Jerry had a slight smile on his lips.

"Wipe that smirk off your face," Jordan said. "It is so Goddamn annoying. You shouldn't take me lightly, I'll tell you that."

"That wasn't how I was planning to take you," Jerry said, holding the lapels of her shirt and pulling her toward him. He turned and pressed her back to the door with his body and started a long slow kiss that grew in passion and intensity. Jordan pulled away, then said, "Oh, hell." She pushed him to the floor, wrestling off his jacket on the way down. Straddling him, she hastily unbuttoned her shirt. "A man with a plan. I love it."

They heard a tap at the door.

"Goddammit, just like high school," she said.

It was Isabelle. "Just a heads up, so to speak," she said through the door. "Cay wants you for something and is coming to get you, Jordan. Thought you might want to know."

Jordan returned to the business at hand. Kissing Jerry was all she had thought it would be and more. His beard stubble scratched just right, and his taste and smell made her dizzy with pleasure. "God I love a man who tastes like old cigarettes," she said.

She stood up and rebuttoned her blouse. Jerry stayed in the floor, looking at her above him. "We aren't leaving this here, you know," he said. "I'm not an easy lay."

Chapter 39

"Cay, would you mind getting the door? My hands are full." Andrea swooped into the living room with a tray of hors 'oeuvres. Lanier was working his magic on a group of Justice Center neighbors, the people Andrea most wanted to win over.

"It says 'Come in' right on the door. Can't they read?" Cay was sitting down for the first time that day, and it felt good. She stood with a sigh and went to the door.

"Well hello, officers. Are you here for the Justice Center Open House? Come in."

"No Ma'am. We need to speak with a Misti Cannon. Is she here?"

"Uh, well, yes and no. She is, sort of. Could you wait right here for a minute?"

As Cay turned to go inside in hope of finding someone else, anyone else, to speak to the police, Jordan poked her head out the front door.

"What's going on out here? Hi, officers. Would you like. . ."

Cay interrupted her. "I don't think this a social call, Jordan. Can you get Lanier? And maybe that new Justice Center lawyer, Jack Gordon. I think both of them might be a good idea."

"Be right back," Jordan nodded at the police officer

and went back inside.

"Could I ask what this is about?" Cay addressed the cop who was now invading her personal space.

"No Ma'am."

"Oh, all righty then, well, I am sure that someone will come to save me – speak to you – in just a minute. This is certainly a nice quiet neighborhood. Bet you don't get much business here, do you?"

The officer shifted his considerable weight to the other foot.

"I'll bet you're tired, aren't you? On your feet all day? I know I have been, and it takes it out of you. It really does." *I sound like an idiot*, Cay thought. *A guilty idiot.*
"Oh, thank the Lord." Cay was so relieved to see Lanier and Jack coming out the door she felt faint. "Well, I leave you in good hands. I'll be going now. Nice to talk with you."

Cay grabbed the first drink off a passing tray. *I don't know what it is, but there are times it doesn't matter.*

"Cay, I never see you drink." Trish surprised her from behind and Cay jumped, spilling half the concoction on her black suede jacket.

"Something is going on out there," Cay said, jerking her head toward the front door. "I have a bad feeling. It's the cops, and it is about Misti. I guess I should find her and tell her. I was in a daze. Police do that to me. I always feel so guilty, like I'm on the lam and they've found me. Swear to God, the first thing I thought when I saw them was 'toaster ovens.'" She downed what little was left in her glass and grimaced. "That's why I don't drink. Now I remember. It tastes like gasoline."

"Don't worry. I'll find Misti. I'm sure she's with Coleman. You just relax."

Cay wanted to find a bed, climb into it, and pull the covers over her head. She settled for an overstuffed club chair in the library. Cay found books comforting, even this odd assortment they had acquired from donations.

"Misti, I have to talk to you. Right now," Trish said, finding Misti in the kitchen.

"Sure, Trish. What's going on?" Misti was arranging a tray of hors d'oeuvres at the kitchen counter, with Coleman right behind her, looking on appreciatively.

"She's a domestic whirlwind," he said. "What an amazing woman."

Pulling Misti aside, Trish said, "The cops are here and they're asking for you. Lanier and Jack are on the front porch talking to them. Before he went out, Lanier told me if they wanted to you-know-what, he'd go in with you. Do you think you need to change into something more, uh, suitable, in case you have to make an appearance at the police department?"

"Heck, no. They've seen party clothes before."

Misti's choice of a skin-tight turquoise leather mini-dress with thigh high black patent boots and fishnet hose would not be on Trish's list for outfits to wear to jail. "I thought for comfort."

"I'm comfortable. Bring it on, I say."

Coleman stepped in front of Misti. "Don't worry your pretty little head. I'm here to defend your honor."

Trish sighed. "Coleman, you're about twenty years too late. That ship has sailed."

Lanier Poole stuck his head in the kitchen. "Misti, I need to speak with you alone. Trish, can we use the office?"

"Of course. I'll unlock it for you," Trish said, as she led the way down the hall.

Misti called back to Coleman over her shoulder. "You just hang on a minute there, Pumpkin, I'll be right back."

As soon as Trish let Misti and Lanier into the office, Cay poked her head out of the library door.

"What's up? What did the police want?"

"I don't know. I'm worried."

Misti and Lanier came out of the office and wove their way through the party without saying a word. Misti's head was down. They stepped outside where Jack Gordon waited with the police.

Cay positioned herself at a library window that looked out on the front porch.

"What do you see?" Trish asked.

Cay peered as far to her right as she could. "They're right up against the door. I can't see much. If they would just step back a little. Where else can I look? I know, there are glass panels on either side of the front door. Maybe we can see there."

Trish shook her head. "No that's too conspicuous. Everyone here would wonder what was going on. So far, the media is concentrating on the celebrity guests here. I guess we'll have to wait."

"In that case, I'm going to get some food," Cay said. "Can I get you something?"

"I couldn't eat a thing," Trish replied. "My stomach is in a knot."

Cay headed back into the party and found Jordan. In a very low voice, Jordan asked, "Do you know what is going on out there?"

"No, and don't say anything to anybody else, especially Andrea. She insisted the Chix turn those keys over to the police, and now it's backfiring on Misti. Andrea would feel terrible. We want her to have a good time, and we don't want anyone else to know the cops have shown up at our door to visit with a resident. That is called bad publicity."

Jack came back inside, followed by Misti and Lanier.

"That's a relief," Jordan said. "At least they didn't haul her away."

Misti joined Jordan and Cay. She was trying to smile but tears were running down her cheeks. They hustled her to the library, hoping no one would notice. "Shit, I wish I could smoke in here," Misti said. "The cops said they came to arrest me for the murder of Lew and a whole shit load of other stuff. Conspiracy, drugs and I don't know what all! I haven't had a cigarette in years, but I sure want one right now."

Jordan put an arm around Misti's shoulders.

"But they didn't arrest you," Cay said. "You're still here."

"That's because of Lanier, bless his heart," Misti said. "He got on his cell phone and called a couple of big shots. They told him someone in the police department screwed up. The district attorney will see us in his office tomorrow morning according to an agreement of some kind, so I can turn myself in. What am I going to do? I didn't really believe it would come to this. At least Lanier's going to go with me. I didn't kill Lew, but the police think I did."

"Misti, this is awful," Cay said. She looked up to see Coleman over her shoulder, holding a cheese straw and a glass of champagne.

"My poor doll baby." he said. "Would a little something make you feel better?" He fed Misti a bite of his hors 'oeuvres.

Andrea appeared at the library door, tray in hand. "Scallops with bacon? A teensy lobster roll? Who knew Mother could make hors d'oeuvres? Why the long faces? C'mon everyone, it's a party. Get out there and mingle!"

Chapter 40

"Ladies, it's late and we would all like to put our feet up, but I really think there is something I should show you before we call it a day." Isabelle said.

"Can't it wait until tomorrow?" Jordan asked. "I have a steamy hot dream waiting for me."

"Since Misti is going to have to face the police tomorrow, I think not. We seem to have a bargaining chip in our possession." Everyone followed Isabelle to her office and crowded around her computer. "Trish asked if I found the name M. Hozk on the USB key, I said I had not. I did however, find a file with an equation for a title. More of a code plus an equation."

"Oh, that sounds like Lew," Misti said. "He loved puzzles and codes and all that kind of stuff."

"The title was very confusing, at first. It said Lapin, which is French for Rabbit. Then I uncovered an arrow pointing to the left, a minus sign and the number one. I played with that for a while trying all different solutions. I concluded the arrow meant to reverse the word. I did that and Lapin became Nipal. Then I started playing with Nipal. To make a long story short, it was a very simple substitution code. If you go backwards one letter for each letter in Nipal, you get Mhozk, or as we have it, M.Hozk.

"Now that file needed its own password." Isabelle smiled. "I was feeling pretty pleased with myself and fortunately the password was obvious. I am surprised Lew didn't come up with a brain teaser, but he didn't: bunny girl. The file was about Misti. It looks as if Lew put the condo - the whole building, all his other real estate, the art, and an amazing amount of cash into Misti's name sometime before they eloped to Vegas. He also has a touching statement where he attests she knows nothing about his business, had no part in it, and doesn't know the source of his funds, etc. So it would seem to me that this little key could be quite useful as a bargaining chip for Misti, naming the names of people in the drug trade all over the world and tracing drug shipments in and out of Atlanta and the Southeast.

If Lew is the Rabbit, and it seems that he is, he is the guilty one, not Misti. It is not a stretch to imagine a drug cartel hired a professional killer to take Lew out. No wonder they are now after Misti if they think she has information that would destroy their network and put so many of them in jail."

The room was silent as each one of them processed this stunning revelation.

"That's good, right? " Misti asked.

"Very, very good." Trish answered. "Isabelle you are amazing. Still we don't have any clue as to how the poor man in the blue sequined dress got the key and why he put it in Misti's make-up bag in Vegas."

"I think there are probably any number of scenarios we could come up with," Isabelle said shutting down the screen, "but I prefer not to speculate. The police will have a field day with all of the material on the key."

"Why did you wait until now to tell us?" Cay asked.

"It was so late last night when I cracked the code and frankly, I didn't expected to need the information so soon," Isabelle said. "This was no easy task for an amateur like me and I wanted to get it right. After all, it was the very last thing on that key I figured out. Until then I was just stumped. With all of the plans for the open house, I wanted to show you the results of my research calmly, so together we could plan how to best use this in exonerating Misti."

"Isabelle, I'm sure Cay wasn't challenging you," Trish said. "You have done fantastic work. None of the rest of us could have worked through this puzzle. In addition to the hours you spent on deciphering the key, you and Mother arranged the party and it was a great success." Everyone nodded in agreement.

Andrea said. "Please go with Misti and the Chix to Lanier's first thing in the morning to explain your findings. I'm sure none of us could tell it so well."

"Of course. It would be my pleasure. Sisterhood is everything, isn't it?" Isabelle beamed.

Chapter 41

"I have another question," Cay said, as she and Jordan were putting leftovers away, "What was that document we just saw? All the information seemed to be financial statements, routes, dealers names. and then there was this really personal statement exonerating Misti. It doesn't seem to fit. Are we sure that document was created by Lew? Could someone else have inserted it, in self interest so to speak, without being detected? If it did come from Lew, why have some Vegas transvestite slip the USB key to Misti? Why didn't Lew give it to her himself? It's just too pat. Misti gets to pass go, collect everything.

"And another thing. Why did Lew use 'bunny girl' to refer to Misti? That was the file password: bunny girl. Jordan, pay attention. I can tell your mind is wandering."

"Sorry, I'm back now. As you were saying?"

"I told you I saw clippings of Misti in a bunny costume before she met Lew. Why do you think he would use bunny girl as a password? The whole thing is suspicious to me. I am having some second thoughts."

Jordan stared for a moment. "To be honest, I'm having trouble giving a shit about Misti. If this key saves the Justice Center and my volunteer job, that's all I care about."

Cay sighed. "Oh, I forgot. Eyes back on Jordan. Can't you try and get over yourself for a minute and think about Misti?"

"I'm still stuck on the fact I almost paid Misti close to half a mil in cash for that condo in Twelve," Jordan said. "Or at least paid that M. Hozk corporation she benefits from. I am so glad Trish talked me out of buying it and found me a new one. At least I have a killer condo with a clean title. It's all mine."

"Well you wanted it, you got it, so enjoy it," Cay said. "I'll pack some of these leftovers to take to your place. I'll also buy some wine. Then, you can invite Trish and Andrea, and have a little house warming."

"I'd like to warm my house, but not with the girls. Don't be offended."

"Don't worry, I'm not. But facts are facts. The girls are all you've got right now. I guess we have to include Misti, Isabelle and Mother. It would be mean to leave them out. Maybe tomorrow night, assuming Misti isn't in the pokey."

"How nice of you two to clean up," Andrea said, entering the kitchen.

"We aren't the only ones who cleaned up, it seems," Cay said. "That document pretty much hands Misti a bloody fortune, doesn't it?"

"She is now a wealthy woman for sure," Andrea said. "I assume it will have to be verified somehow. It doesn't completely answer the question of Lew's murder. There are still problems to solve. However it does seem to clear Misti of any involvement in the drug end of Lew's business. We were just talking in the office. Mother suggested Misti agree to give the police or the feds or whoever the key in exchange for immunity from prosecution. A lot of drug cases will be solved with the material on that key. A major source and suppliers of drugs will be put out of business or at least crippled as well."

"Mother has a law degree, too?" Cay said. "Will the old gal's areas of expertise never quit? Say, couldn't the authorities just take the key as evidence if they want to?"

"Well, Isabelle said Misti should give the key to Lanier so he can cover possession with client-attorney privilege. Between Isabelle and Mother, Misti is in much better shape than she was," Andrea said. "Of course she didn't kill Lew, but proof is normally difficult when you're innocent."

"You're right," Jordan said. "Innocent people don't usually have everything laid so neatly on a computer key. I'm surprised there was not a statement saying, 'P.S. If I turn up dead, Misti didn't kill me. Sincerely, Lew."

Andrea laughed. "Jordan, you are such a cynic."

"Thank you," she said.

Chapter 42

"Ow! Watch it," Misti squirmed on the sofa while a policewoman fastened a wide black band around her left ankle. After an adjustment with a little screwdriver, she asked, "How does that feel?"

"Oh, wonderful. Love it. How in the hell do you think it feels? Like shit, that's how."

"Stand up. Put your weight on your left foot," the policewoman asked. "Too tight?"

"No, I guess it's as good as it's going to get," Misti said.

"Thank you officer," Andrea said, walking her to the door. "I'm sure you'll be back in a day or two to remove it." The policewoman nodded crisply, got in her cruiser and left.

"Oh, the neighbors, the neighbors," Andrea said as she closed the door. "I wish we didn't have so many black and whites in our front yard."

Andrea's cell rang. "Jordan, hi. We just got back from Lanier's. We have good news. What? I can't understand you. Talk more slowly. Where are you? What? *What*? Jordan, what's wrong? Are you crying? Is there someone there who can tell me what is going on? I can't understand a word you are saying."

There was a brief pause and the speaker changed to Detective Bongiovanni.

"Jerry? What happened? Is Jordan all right?" Andrea knew her voice was shrill and panicked but she couldn't help it. Her hands shook so badly she could hardly hold her cell. "Wait. She found what in her condo? Are you serious? Who is he? How can we help? Of course. We'll be waiting for her. Thanks for your kindness."

Jerry apparently handed the phone back to Jordan, who continued to weep loudly. "Jordan! Jordan! Hang in there, Jordan. We'll see you in a few minutes. Everything will be all right, Sweetie. Let the police bring you to the Justice Center. We'll get through this together." Andrea shut her cell cover.

"What was that all about?" Misti asked, practicing walking with the heavy bracelet on her ankle. "How am I going to wear fishnets with this thing?" she said.

"You wear these," Andrea said, holding up a pair of white cotton socks the policewoman left. "These and flats or sneakers are about it. Heels are very uncomfortable with ankle bracelets. "

"Eeeuuw, disgusting," Misti said. "I haven't worn flats since I was practically a baby. Anyway, what happened to Jordan?"

"She found a dead man in her condo, freaked out and the police are bringing her over here."

"A body?" Misti asked, brightening a little. "Just like me. We'll have something common; both of us had killers in our condos. Say, maybe I can help clear her like you all helped me."

Trish and Cay rushed into the hall. Trish said, "What's happening Andrea? We heard you talking to Jordan. Is she OK?"

Andrea said, "She's as fine as you can be with a dead body in her condo. Jerry's with her and a policeman is bringing her here."

"Omigod," said Cay. "A dead body? Man or woman?"

Andrea replied, "Man. At least I think that's what she said. Poor Jordan. She was hysterical and I don't blame her. What a shock."

Trish headed back to the kitchen. "I'll start a pot of coffee and see if the snicker brownies are done. I put them in the oven about twenty minutes ago Nothing like caffeine and chocolate when you are upset."

Misti let out an expletive as she pulled up the white socks. "How long do I have to wear these frigging things? They are so damn tacky."

Andrea stared at Misti. "About that bracelet. You know it will beep if you get too far away from the base monitor right? That basically means that you can't go farther than ten or fifteen feet outside the walls of the Center. You can go from the attic to the basement, and around the immediate outside, but not off the property."

"As if I would want to go to the basement ever again," Misti said. "It still gives me chills to think about that weird guy and how close we came to being dead meat."

"I'm sure it won't be long before Lanier and the D.A. get the terms of your agreement worked out. Then it will be signed off on by a judge and you will be able to take that ankle bracelet off. Look on the bright side: you aren't in jail in the meantime. When there is a murder the authorities get very testy about letting someone out for any reason. We are so lucky Lanier helped you."

"Lanier is so cool," Misti said. "Is he married? You ought to go after him, Andrea. I'll bet you could catch him."

"No thanks," Andrea laughed ruefully. "Lanier loves Lanier too much."

"We'll make Jordan feel so much better when she gets here," Misti said. "We can tell her Lanier stood right up to that DA and said I wouldn't give them the key until they dropped all charges against me, including Lew's murder. That key thingy is in a little brown paper bag in Lanier's safe. Attorney-client privilege is the best thing ever! I'm going to call Coleman. He said he's gonna come over and fix me a very special dinner. That's OK, isn't it?"

"Yes, of course it is. You and Coleman are really hitting it off, aren't you?"

"Yeah, we are. I never thought such a fine gentleman would be interested in me, but I think he is. In the real me. Oh, Hi, Trish."

Trish came into the living room pushing the tea caddy with coffee, cups and a platter of snicker brownies. "How's the ankle bracelet?"

"Lousy, but Andrea says I won't have to wear it for long. In the meantime, I am going to think positively. Andrea says we have to get in the habit of positive thinking to make our dreams a reality. Oh, speaking of dreams, Coleman is coming over soon and he makes me happy."

"Misti, about Coleman," Trish said.

"What about Coleman?" Misti asked. "Do you think I'm not good enough for him? You think he's too ritzy for the likes of me?"

"No, no, that's not it at all. It's just that the family has always thought Coleman was a little, what shall I say, light in the loafers? He's forty-five and still living with his Mother. Never had a girlfriend we've known about, and well, look at him."

"Look at what? I think he looks like the cover of one of those men's magazines. Not the ones with the muscle guys, but the ones with rich guys in classy suits. I'll be the one to decide if Coleman is queer, and I guarantee you my method is a lot more sure fire than any of your up-tight Florida relatives' bitchy remarks. They're probably just jealous."

Mother came into the living room. "I think there is a police car, outside. I saw the lights in the office."

Andrea said. "They had to use the lights? Oh, for heaven's sake. Two cop cars in one morning. The neighbors are going to come after us with pitchforks and torches." She opened the front door. Jordan, propped on the arm of a police officer, her hair and clothes in disarray, came in and collapsed on the sofa in the living room, exactly where Misti had landed not long before when she had fled her condo.

Trish sat by her and gave her a hug. "Jordan, for heaven's sake, are you all right? Poor Baby. Do you need something to drink?"

Mother said, "I know just the thing," and hurried off, only to return with a small glass. "This is a good stiff toddy, and it will fix you up. Drink it right down, now. No sipping. It has to hit your system and give it a good shake to do any good. Good thing I keep my flask handy."

Jordan did as Mother suggested and downed the liquor in one gulp. Cay brought a soft afghan throw from the library and put it around Jordan's shoulders.

Trish said, "Poor thing. You are shaking so hard, honey." She turned to the group. "Do you think she's in shock?"

"Of course she's in shock," Andrea said. "She needs to go to bed. Somebody get some pillows and she can sleep right here. I can close the curtains and make the room nice and dark. When she wakes up she can tell us what happened."

Jordan shook her head. "No. It'll help me to talk about it. I was getting the condo ready for our get together tonight. I needed some cleaning supplies and remembered there were some in the utility closet. Where's my chapstick? I need my chapstick." Andrea ran out to the entry hall and found one in Jordan's purse.

"Anyway," Jordan said, stopping to run the chapstick over her lips two or three times, "I tried to open the closet door and it wouldn't budge. I looked for a key in the stuff the realtor gave me, but I couldn't find it, so I used the old credit card method to pop the door, and I went inside, and there, and there..."

"Take your time, Sugar," Trish said.

"It was dark inside, so I found the light switch, and there he was - slumped on the floor. I couldn't see his face because there was some kind of dark hood over his head. It was the one we saw in front of Misti's condo. Remember? It said 'M. Hozk and Company.' It was over the parking meter. Right in the middle of his chest, there was a knife sticking through a piece of paper. '3 K' was written on it in blood. Big writing. There was so much friggini' blood all over the place. I speed dialed Jerry. The next thing I knew cops were all over the condo. Jerry put me in the back of a police car. He got in with me and just let me cry on his shoulder. It was almost worth it. He is the best smelling man on the planet. If they could bottle that combination of tobacco and male musk and..."

"Jordan, get back on track," Cay said. "Did the police tell you anything? Like who the man was or why he was in your condo?"

"Nothing, or at least I don't remember anything. What does '3 K' mean, for God's sake, and why did he have on that horrible hood?"

"You don't know that?" Mother spoke up. "3 K, that's baseball. Three strikes."

"Three strikes and you're out," Trish said softly.

"Exactly."

"The killer must have failed at something three times," Trish said. "He must have followed us to the condo when we went to get Misti's pocket book. That's where the hood came from. He was leaving someone a message." She shuddered.

"Yeah," Misti said. "Maybe the message was for him. He missed killing me three times. First, there was the explosion at the Yoga Studio. If I hadn't been late, I could have been killed there. Then, maybe he was supposed to get me at the condo and Lew surprised him instead, that's two. Then there were Jordan's brakes failing when I was supposed to be in her car. That hardly sounds like a hit, but it could have been, I guess. But what about the intruder? I thought he just wanted the key, but that might count as another attempt."

"Don't forget the drive-by when you were shopping on Buford Highway," Trish said, "Wouldn't that be number four?"

"Maybe the murderer doesn't count too well," Cay said. "Or maybe there was more than one hit... hit persons."

"Oh, that's reassuring," Jordan said and blew her nose.

"Well, it would seem this was a killing for sure," Trish said. "This man's killer needed a place to stash the body. It's obvious the killer was leaving a message where it was sure to get to Misti. Could this be a mob killing? What if this was the hit man who was hired to take Misti out. Failure isn't rewarded in those circles." Trish frowned. "Jordan, my advice is get new locks everywhere."

"Are you kidding?" Jordan said. "The security at Fort Knox won't be as elaborate as my new system. But, why me? If the killer wants to leave a message, he could use the phone."

Jordan shrugged off the afghan, "Changing the subject, I just told Jim I bought my own place. I told him I was going to move into it this week."

"What did he say?" Trish asked.

"He cried," Jordan said. "That sure took the wind out of my sails."

"Did you ask your son if he wanted to live there

with you, if he decides to go to Georgia Tech next fall?"
Andrea asked.

"Yeah. He said something sensitive like 'Hell no.'
That time I was the one who cried."

The front door opened. Isabelle called, "Yoo hoo.
Anybody here?"

"We're in the living room," Andrea said.

"I want to hear all about the police coming to see
Misti this morning." She stopped at the threshold and
studied the group. "Is something else going on? Why the
long faces?"

Mother stood. "Sit down, Isabelle. I'll go get
another toddy for you. When you hear what happened,
you'll need it."

Chapter 43

"They say Atlanta is the prettiest place in the world when the dogwoods bloom," Coleman said. "I believe it. Piedmont Park is one of my favorite spots, especially in the spring. Having the Dogwood Festival here is the perfect location. I love the art, the entertainment, the good food and the eclectic crowd. Most of all, I love being here with you Misti." They were walking among the white canvas tents spread out under the trees stopping now and again to examine something more closely.

"It's pretty fuckin' beautiful, all right. Oops, sorry Coleman. Pardon my French. I forget I'm speaking to a gentleman."

"I don't mind Misti. I really don't. That's your native speech. I find it charming. The first time I met you, I thought you were one hundred percent natural and genuine. Everyone is always trying to be somebody else. Not you. You are just Misti."

A few petals from the dogwoods drifted down and clung to Misti' bare shoulders. "This is the perfect place to celebrate getting rid of that damn ankle bracelet. I feel so free," and she danced a few steps around Coleman. Misti took Coleman's hand. "You have the softest hands. What did you say you do for a living?"

"I didn't say, really."

"That's OK. Don't be embarrassed. I've known people who do everything. And I do mean everything. As long as your heart is good and you're not abusive, what you do doesn't matter. At least that's what I think."

Taking a deep breath, Coleman said, "Well, it's like this. My Grandfather had the presence of mind to invest in some Florida real estate near Orlando that wasn't too attractive at the time, but, well, it improved, rather dramatically. After graduating from Harvard, I moved into the family home with Mother and entertained myself with books and music and tinkering around in the basement. I listen to opera while I work on inventions. Maybe you'd like to go with me to the opera sometime. You might like it."

"The opera? No one's ever asked me to go to the opera before, that's for damn sure. That's really sweet of you, Coleman." Misti planted a kiss on his cheek. He turned to her and placed his hands gently on either side of her face. He drew her closer and gave her a long kiss, so full of yearning that Misti surprised herself by kissing him back.

"Coleman! You are a good kisser! I mean, we've kissed before, a little, but not like this." Misti moved in, wrapped both her arms and one leg around him and gave him a kiss that would have earned an R rating. When she finally let him go, her top was nearly turned backwards. Coleman was breathless and had lost his glasses.

"My goodness," Coleman gasped. His chest was heaving. "That was quite spectacular, Misti."

"Oh, honey, you ain't seen nothing yet."

Standing eye to eye with Misti, he looked even smaller than she did. He snatched Misti off her feet and carried her to a nearby stone bench under an umbrella of white dogwood blossoms. He placed her on his lap and stroked her cheek. "Misti, I think you are just about the most adorable thing I have ever seen in my entire life. Would you allow me to court you?"

"What' me? Oh you mean date me? We've gone way past dating already, you hot baby. I am going to show you some things you never saw at the opera, I can promise you that." She grasped a handful of his fine, pale hair, pulled his head back and launched an assault on his mouth. He stopped her just as she was working her way south.

"Oh, my dear, we are going to get ourselves arrested if this goes much farther. The park police are quite strict. I think we need to find another venue, as it were." His voice was muffled by desire and by Misti's breasts which were pressed against his face. "This could get embarrassing quite soon."

"I'm not embarrassed by anything," Misti said. "This is good old fashioned animal magnetism." She undulated against him with the force of her pole dancing experience.

"Shit, what's that?" Misti pulled back and put her hand to the side of her face.

"Well, my sweet cupcake, I should think you would know what 'that' is," Coleman said, pulling her back against him.

"No. Look!" She held up her hand, which was covered in blood. "Something stung me. It hurts like hell." She scrambled off of Coleman.

"Omigod. It's your ear." Coleman pulled out a handkerchief. He reached up to dab it. "Your earring has been torn out. Misti, you've got to get to a doctor." He sat Misti on the bench beside him and began to adjust his clothes. There was a rush of air and a spray of tree bark flew between.

"Holy shit! Somebody's shooting at us. Run Coleman, run! You go to the left! Now!" Misti gave him a shove.

They sprinted in different directions, leaping over ropes securing the tents that housed artists and crafts people. They dodged in and out between displays and food vendors. Misti stopped for moment behind a cotton candy wagon and spotted her pursuer, a tall man in a dark shirt and pants, a contrast to the pastels of the Festival goers. She began to run again, zigzagging between the tents and trees, dodging a glass blower, until she came to the tile and brick building housing some restrooms. She ducked into one with a sign outside that said 'Out of Order.'

Chapter 44

"Damnedest thing I ever saw," the GBI investigator said, shaking his head and wiping his forehead with a handkerchief. His walkie-talkie burst to life and he shouted directions to the voice at the other end. He turned to the Atlanta police around him. "The victim is in there," and he nodded toward the quaint brick and tile building housing restrooms. "Shot himself. Twice. Right in the heart. You work in this business long enough you'll see everything, I guess. Get the crowd and those damned reporters back behind the yellow tape."

Two rookie cops faced the crowd. One of them shouted, "Crime scene folks, move back please. There is nothing to see, so go back to what you were doing."

"Do you know who the victim is?" an arriving reporter shouted.

Another reporter thrust his microphone in the policeman's face. "Was this a protest of some sort? An anti-festival freak?"

"No idea, but that's for the detectives to determine. That's all. No comment. Move away please."

The reporter faced his cameraman and spoke into his WSB microphone, "The Atlanta Dogwood Festival has been interrupted by violence. An unidentified victim was shot and killed with his own gun in a closed restroom.

We'll be reporting more information as we receive it. Back to you Monica."

Misti sat on a bench next to Coleman, a blanket around her shoulders and a gauze bandage over her ear. A policewoman listened to her story and took notes.

"It was such a beautiful day to be in the park with my sweetie until this awful thing happened. When we realized someone was shooting as us, we ran as fast as we could. Coleman went one way and I went the other. I realized I couldn't outrun the man so I ducked into the rest room to hide. It had one of those cones outside that said it was closed and I guess I thought I'd be safe. I realized that was really dumb because there was only the one door and I was trapped, but you don't think in situations like that, you know? You just react.

"Lucky for me the floor was wet and when that fucker - I mean person – ran in behind me, he slipped and fell, right on his gun. I heard it go off, but I thought he was shooting at me again."

"So you think he was shooting at you specifically?" The policewoman asked.

"Well, he followed me and not Coleman," she turned to Coleman. "This is giving me a headache."

"Misti can give a more thorough report at your headquarters later." Coleman said, with surprising authority. He stood, taking Misti's arm, helping her to get up. "She has had a horrifying experience and needs to rest. If you have no reason to detain her further, I'm taking her to the Women's Justice Center where she is staying at present. You can get in touch with her there after we consult with her lawyer, Lanier Poole."

* * *

"Where is Misti, anyway?" Cay asked. "Is she all right?"

"I think she's going to be fine," Andrea said. "Still a little jumpy, but she said she was going to take a long hot bath and I saw Coleman carrying some bath towels, so I'd say all is well. I'm glad you're here, Jerry. You make us all feel more secure."

Jerry nodded. "When I heard the scanner, I knew it was one of you. Just knew it. Couldn't be anyone else. Misti will have to make a full statement tomorrow. Probably a good idea to lawyer up, just in case she's inclined to say more than she should.

"I think the scenario is pretty clear." Jerry went on. "Whoever is after her obviously doesn't know Misti no longer has the USB key. My guess is that either they want to get it back, or they want to be sure the information on it doesn't get out. As soon as the DA makes his televised speech about having the USB key with all kinds of data on it about drug trafficking in Atlanta – worldwide, in fact- Misti shouldn't be a target.

"Oh, another thing you may find interesting. Sorry to bring this up, Jordan. The guy in Jordan's condo was a contract killer for the Russian mob. He had something on his face that turned out to be saliva. Male DNA again, just like Lew. I don't mind telling you we do not have that one figured out but we got a match. The same man whacked both vics. You can bet we are going to check the guy from the park today. Enough pieces of the puzzle and you can eventually figure it out."

"I need a drink," Cay said, "and I wasn't even there. I'm going to the kitchen for iced tea. Anyone want some?"

"I'll come with you," Andrea stood up. "Jerry? Jordan? You want anything? Jerry? Jordan? Oh, never mind. Isabelle. Hey. I didn't hear you come in. Have you heard about the big excitement?"

"Indeed I have. What a shocking story. Misti told me all about it while I was getting her a bottle of Clorox."

"Clorox? Wasn't her tub clean?"

"Oh she doesn't use it on the tub. She wanted it for herself. She said a good scrub with diluted Clorox once in a while is what gives her skin a glossy look. A dynamite exfoliatant, apparently, if you sprinkle it in the water like bath oil. Sounds like it would take the skin right off, to me, but I'm no beauty expert. And the smell!" She poured sweet tea into her glass. "She said Coleman, well, let's just say she indicated the smell appeals to Coleman in an erotic way."

"Hmm, nice little treatment for gun powder residue, too," Cay muttered.

"Cay! Really. They said the man pursuing Misti shot himself," Andrea said. "There shouldn't be gunpowder on Misti."

"Just saying..." Cay said. She filled her glass and sat at the kitchen counter. "Say! Do we have any snicker-brownies left? I'm starved."

Chapter 45

Misti sat down in a chair in the WJC administrative office where Trish was working on the volunteer list. "Hey, girl. Glad you're here alone." She crossed her legs. "Tell me more about Coleman. I don't know much about him and the little twerp's growing on me in a big way.. We've been together almost every day since we met at church.

Trish put down her pen and picked up her coffee mug. "I'm so glad you brought that up. I've been wondering about whether y'all are getting serious. Coleman is my cousin, but he's also my friend. He's very important to me and I don't want him to be hurt. You rushed into marriage with Lew, and that didn't work out all that well for him."

Misti sat up straighter in the chair, "Oh for God's sake what happened to Lew wasn't my fault! I'm just the kind of girl who falls hard and fast. Always have been. I knew so little about Lew, I don't want to make the same mistake."

"OK, what can I tell you? I never asked him about his sex life. He was so much fun and a great dancer. All the girls loved him, but he was never very interested in any of them. They always took him shopping with them because he has such impeccable taste, and really knows how to dress a woman. None of that means he's gay, so I don't know what to tell you. Guess you'll have to find out first hand if you really want to know."

"OK, then it's up to me to make the first move. Got it. Now, next question, is he rich? And if so, how rich? I found out I like to have a nice lifestyle."

Trish leaned across the desk, "If this matters to you, Misti, ask him. He inherited some money and has done well with his personal investments and as an inventor. Besides, if you really care about him, money shouldn't matter, Misti."

"Inventor? He said something about tinkering in his basement and inventing stuff, but I didn't realize he was a real honest-to-God inventor!"

"Well, Coleman is modest about his personal achievements. He made top grades at Harvard, got his degree in nuclear engineering. I know he possesses patents on several military inventions, but they are very top-secret, so no one knows exactly what they are."

Misti seemed pleased with Trish's explanation. "OK. How about his mother? Would she totally disapprove of me?"

"Aunt Kate? No, she is a hoot! However outrageous she acts, she is too rich for the local society to snub. I can't predict her reaction to anything, and that's a fact. I don't think you have to worry about Aunt Kate. She has wanted Coleman to marry for years. He is her only child and she wants an heir." Trish smiled.

"OK, last question. Coleman has told me Lake City is a small town, but how provincial is it? If Coleman and I promise to 'love, honor, and obey' and all that shit, not that I believe we will, I want to open an exercise studio using my pole dancing. That way I can keep in shape and help other ladies lose weight and get stronger. Would there be enough women there to make it successful?" Misti smiled. "I want to call it The Pole Position. Wha'cha think?"

Fortunately for her, Trish didn't have to answer. Cay walked in with an armful of donated books. She was organizing the library in the next room, and wanted a fresh opinion.

"Hey, Misti. Glad you're here. I wanted to ask you something. Can you help me in the library?" Cay put the books on a side table.

"Sure. Thanks for our little talk, Trish. Let's keep it to ourselves, OK?" Misti asked. She left the room with Cay and walked down the hall to the library.

"Man, there's a shitload of books here. Who's gonna read all this stuff?" Misti stood with her hands on her hips.

Cay smiled and said, "Could you put them on the shelves in alphabetical order by author." She rolled a cart loaded with books to the first empty shelf.

Cay heard Misti humming the Alphabet Song and saw her putting the books in order. Cay had her in the self-help section hoping she would find a title that captured her attention, such as it was.

"Misti, it's really none of my business, but when Trish, Jordan, and I were in your condo, I saw some scrapbooks on the bookshelves and you were in some pictures that looked like they were taken in Vegas. Why did you get upset? Were you in Vegas before you married Lew?"

Misti stopped sorting. "That's kinda private, don't you think?"

"Remember, we were trying to find something to help clear you of Lew's murder. I didn't mean to pry, but since we didn't know exactly what we were looking for, I was examining everything that might give us a clue."

Misti teared up. "Lew had those made up for me." She wiped her eyes with the back of her hand. "I had this big ol' box of clippings and he thought I'd be really pleased if he put them in leather scrapbooks for me. He was so sweet. Anyway, I guess he didn't realize the only thing I wanted to do was forget those days. I never tell anyone I was in Vegas before we got married. You see," Misti snuffled and reached in her bra for a tissue, "I had to get out of my house really young. Like fifteen. Things were bad, really bad, at home. This guy got me a job in Vegas and I was lucky he wasn't a pimp. I was so dumb about everything. He got me a fake I.D. and put me in a show. Then, all of a sudden I was making money."

"You don't have to explain anything. I'm sorry if I brought back bad memories."

Misti smiled. "Well, it wasn't all bad. But, as soon as I had a little dough saved up, I was outta there. I didn't really like Vegas. That life was too fast for me. Once I got to Atlanta, it just felt right, you know. Not too big, not too small. I wanted to forget those early days so I never tell anyone I was ever there. Now, when I think of Vegas, I think of Lew and our wedding, so that's a good memory."

"Sorry, I said anything about it. I saw a picture of you in a bunny costume, and I was curious. It must have been an Easter show, if they celebrate holidays like that in Vegas."

Misti said, "I don't remember that." She walked toward the library door. "Coleman is taking me to lunch and I need to change my clothes. I want to forget about the past and make some new, hot memories with Coleman. See ya later."

Cay sighed and started re-alphabetizing the books Misti worked on.

Chapter 46

The sideboard in the Justice Center was decorated with pink camellias from the blooming shrubs outside. On the dining room table blue hydrangeas, gardenias and magnolia blossoms combined with baby's breath, English ivy and acuba leaves created a towering floral center piece. Jordan and Cay were putting the finishing touches on wisteria swags. Isabelle and Mother were cooking in the kitchen for the Misti's wedding the next day while Trish was leaving notes all over the dining table to identify which dishes were to be placed in each location.

"Misti, I can't tell you how happy we are that you've found love again," Andrea said. "I know you don't want a bachelorette party, but is there anything we can do tonight to celebrate your wedding in the morning?"

"You've done so much already. All of you," Misti said. "I've been a lot of trouble, haven't I?"

"Yes, you have," Jordan said. There was a pause followed by laughter. "However, without you, I would never have had so many chances to see Jerry, and the LitChix wouldn't have been able to sleuth so much. All our discussions about crime scenes and solving murders in our book club have sure come in handy."

Misti glanced around at the group now assembled in the entry hall. "I think, if nobody minds, I would like to spend sometime by myself this evening, just thinking about things. Tomorrow I'll be a married woman, but tonight I'm just me, and I want to think about where I've been and where I'm going."

"Misti, that is so mature of you," Trish said. "What wonderful idea."

"Would it be possible to build a fire in the fireplace in the library? It's a chilly spring night and I'll put it out before I go to bed. A fire always helps me think."

Andrea nodded. "I'll ask Jackson to lay a fire in the library and get it started whenever you like, Misti. I think we all need an early night. Tomorrow is going to be a very busy day."

* * *

Misti pulled her dressing table chair into her closet, stood on it and reached her pink suitcase. Lowering it to the floor, she took the little gold key she kept in her jewelry box, opened it up, and pulled out one of the leather bound scrapbooks. After everything was back in place, she carried the book quietly downstairs to the library and sat cross legged in front of the fire. Opening the embossed cover, she began to flip slowly through the book, stopping from time to time to pull out a page or an envelope and set them aside. Most were documents or articles, with only an occasional picture, beginning nearly thirty years before. A birth certificate for Mikel Lapin, a school picture of a little boy, a tooth missing, 'Mikel age 7' written on the back in pencil, and then some medical records. Records from clinics, hospitals, mostly in Canada. The words 'sexual reassign-ment candidate.' Then a blurry photograph of a young woman in front of an anonymous office building , with 'Misti Lapin' penciled on the back.'

One by one, the scraps of paper went into the fire. Misti's eyes shone with tears that didn't fall. She stirred the fire several times, added more wood, then carried the rest of her scrapbook upstairs. She returned it to the suitcase and got ready for bed. Tomorrow she was starting a new life …again.

Chapter 47

"Cay! You have legs – who knew?" Jordan secured a swag of ivy and stared at Cay. "I thought we'd be treated to Birks with some wedding bell patterned socks. This is quite a surprise."

"Of course I have legs. What's that supposed to mean? Here, take one of these." Cay handed Jordan one of the two large Art Nouveau vases filled with velvety purple iris she picked from her garden. "Put it on one end of the mantle."

"I just mean I haven't seen you in a dress in ages. You look beautiful. And real shoes! You pulled out all the stops."

Cay knew the Diane von Furstenberg wrap dress flattered her. Wearing a dress felt good for a change, but the blue peep-toe heels were another matter. They would come off before the day was over.

"I think I have changed my career plans," Jordan said, helping Cay put the matching vase and flowers at the other end of the mantle. She stepped back and turned the vases for the best effect. "I thought I wanted to stage houses and condos to sell, but now I think I want to be a wedding planner instead." Jordan stepped back to admire the effect. "See, Misti and Coleman will be married right here, in front of the fireplace."

"From the looks of this place, you could do a great job. Jordan, this is nothing short of amazing. As Trish and Andrea say: 'you done good' and without spending a fortune. Seems to me you have a lot of latent talent in decorating."

"The lavender wisteria and ivy do work well with your iris, don't they. Oh, it really is pretty, isn't it?"

"Yes it is, Jordan." Cay gave her a hug.

"Jordan, Cay, come up here." Trish beckoned them from top of the stairs. "You have to see Misti."

Andrea turned one bedroom of the Justice Center into a guest room and filled it with a canopy bed covered in red and cream toile. The spread and the matching drapes were brought from Chateau Soleil. They were perfect with the carved mahogany four poster bed belonging to her grandparents. Misti was looking at herself in the antique pier glass in the corner, next to a window.

Cay said. "With the light shining on you like that, you look like an angel. Really truly, you do. Not one of those flimsy angels in white robes but a Medieval angel in gold. A warrior angel, Saint Michael the Archangel, female version. Whoa, where did that come from? I meant it in a good way."

"All you need are wings." Trish said as she stepped closer to examine the short gold lace dress Misti wore.

"Isn't this something? Andrea got it for me. It's my something new even though it was sold on Craig's List. It fits as if it were designed for me."

"Calvin Klein," Andrea said. "Can't go wrong." Cap sleeves and a wide square neckline showed off Misti's trim but muscular arms and strong neck. Her breasts were elevated but without being too exposed. She wore flat Grecian style Jimmy Choo sandals of gold leather with the narrow cords wrapped and tied around her ankles.

"You don't think these shoes are too flat, do you? I mean, Coleman wouldn't care if I wore six inch platforms.

But I sort of wanted to be about the same height as he is today."

"They are perfect," Jordan said. "And I know shoes."

"Are you going to wear a veil?" Cay asked.

"No. I never really got the veil thing, you know? I think the bride and groom need to get a good look at each other. One of the girls I knew from Cheetah II loaned me this." She lifted an ornate headband with gold and crystal leaves out of a hat box. "She did this really classy Greek goddess number and she wore this. It's the only thing she didn't take off. She knew how much I liked it. Wasn't that sweet?"

"Who would have thunk it?" Cay said. "It's exquisite."

"Well, strippers can have expensive taste," Misti said. "She did this Olympic tribute with hoola hoops, you know, like the Olympic rings – you cannot believe what that woman could do with a hula hoop."

"Let's not go there," Cay said. "I have a feeling that I would have to carry that image with me to my grave."

"So I guess that is 'something borrowed,'" Trish said.

"And old, too," Misti added. "I think it's an antique." She settled the wreath into her cap of white gold curls.

"That just leaves something blue. Do you have anything blue?" Jordan asked.

"Well, if you count violet, then my bouquet is blue. I wasn't even going to carry flowers but Andrea said I should have a bouquet to throw, so she got me this," and Misti pointed to a bunch of violets tied with purple and gold ribbons in a florist box on the dressing table.

"Perfect," Jordan said. "I couldn't have done better myself."

"Oh, and I have blue in my sapphire and diamond ring. "

"I hope you got a big one. Coleman can afford it," Trish said.

"He told me I could have anything I wanted, but I wanted the ring his Momma offered me. It belonged to her Grandmother, and it is worn thin in places. There are chips of diamonds and sapphires around a center diamond. Inside the band is an inscription, 'Love Forever 1885.' You can hardly read it. Isn't that the sweetest thing? They were together for over fifty years. If it was good enough for her, it's good enough for me."

"You didn't get an engagement ring, did you?" Cay asked.

"I didn't want one. I don't like a lot of jewelry. I don't know why. It just doesn't appeal to me, you know?"

"No, I don't know," Jordan said. "I can't imagine it."

"How are you and Coleman's mother getting along, anyway?" Cay asked.

"Good. I'm surprised, because I thought she would be all uptight and hanging onto him and all, but she said she's glad he's getting married. She's giving us the home place and is buying a condo so she can travel worry-free. She's so cute and vivacious. She wants to invest money in my exercise studio. She says this will help the women of Lake City to lose weight and develop self-confidence along with muscles."

"What is a great idea." Cay said. "Dance with a pole and reshape your outlook on life. Downright philosophical and life-changing. It just might work."

Trish hugged Misti. "I feel a little teary. We are going to be cousins now."

"Cay, Coleman and I both are so excited you are going to marry us." Misti gave Cay a hug.

"I am too, but I'm a little nervous. This is so special with family and all. Look at your wedding certificate." Cay pulled a parchment out of an envelope. "It almost looks like a Medieval piece of art. The wisteria and iris twine into the letters of your names. Jordan designed it."

"Omigod. Cay it's breathtaking. I'll frame it and hang it where I can see it every day. And look. The flowers are just like the ones you brought for the mantle.

"Just dumb luck," Cay said. "Oh dear God, I completely forgot to remind you, Do either of you have your marriage license? I have to file it with the clerk of the court within three days to have your marriage legally registered."

"I've got it," said Misti. "Trish, you and Jordan look at this." She passed them the certificate.

Jordan said, "This turned out really beautiful. Cay, you continually surprise me. Look at you." Cay was wearing a cream colored robe with a stole in blue, lavender and green. "Very nice. We make a darn good team if I do say so. My decorating is tasteful and you make a great officiant. Maybe we should go into business together."

"An interesting but scary thought," Cay said.

Andrea stepped into the room. "I think it's time everyone went downstairs," she dabbed her own eyes with a tissue. "This is such a special occasion. It's the Justice Center's first wedding. We've been through a lot in a short time. Be sure to have one of my special drinks. Waiters will be passing trays after the ceremony."

Jordan said, "You and your special drinks, Andrea. What is it this time? Remember the Panther Piss martini you served …oh, well, I guess that's not a good memory, is it?"

"I know, we served it at our last party, Sonny's and mine. That seems like a million years ago. I call this drink 'The Blushing Bunny.' Pink since that is Misti's favorite color. Of course we have champagne if people want that, but the Blushing Bunny is delicious – sort of like a strawberry daiquiri with ice cream and rum. I'll see y'all downstairs."

Chapter 48

The most conservative of Lake City met the girls of Cheetah II in the wisteria swaged living room of the Women's Justice Center. It was a tie as to who found the other more exotic. Coleman's Lake City relatives did what the well-to-do usually do in an awkward social situation: they ignored it, in the confidence that it would soon go away.

The girls of Cheetah II exuded confidence as well. They knew how many potential customers there were among the wedding guests, men they would see a few weeks from now, who would stuff bills in their G-strings and say, "Remember me? From Misti's wedding." They would smile and say "Of course I do, darlin'," although they didn't. "Why don't I give you a very special lap dance right after this set?" You could take that to the bank.

Lanier gave Misti away. Candles flickering from the mantle illuminated Misti's golden dress and headband. She had no attendants. "I couldn't choose," she said. Mr. Chanel was the ring bearer, with the rings tied with a gold ribbon to his blue rhinestone collar.

The service was short and mostly traditional. The Bride and Groom pledged with original vows, but only Coleman promised to obey. When the young violinist launched into *Ode to Joy* everyone exited the living room for the reception in the dining room and entry hall.

Coleman scooted up to Trish. "Isn't Misti the most beautiful thing you have ever seen? How can I ever thank you for introducing my Honey Bunny to me? It's like a miracle."

"The Bunny thing just keeps on going," Trish shook her head and hugged Coleman tightly.

Coleman beamed. "Well, you've seen the pictures of Misti's famous Bunny costume, I assume. That big puffy while tail, and not a whole lot more." He nudged Trish in the ribs and giggled. "That was during what she calls her Vegas years. She was quite a star, I'd say."

"No, actually, I haven't seen those pictures," Trish said. "I'll have to ask her about them."

"Oh, don't do that. She made me promise not to tell, and I've been a bad boy. She says this is a whole new life for her, and she wants her past to just disappear." He turned to greet a guest from Lake City.

Trish watched him and thought, *The Rabbit. That's what it said on the USB key giving the financial details of the crime cartel dealing heroin to the Southeastern United States. Isabelle read enough Cyrillic to pick that out. The Southeast was run by The Rabbit, who was controlled from Vegas. The police determined Lew had to be The Rabbit. Misti even called him Bunny Boy. The evidence of the drug trade filled the condo right below Lew's, the condo that...Misti now owned. Lew gave her condo building. What if...No,* Trish shook her head. *I am not even going to consider that. Lew was a bad guy, Lew is dead, and Misti was cleared of his murder. He knew too much, and she didn't know anything. That's what the authorities said and that is what I am going to believe.* She straightened her shoulders and began talking to the guests with her usual hospitality and cheerful demeanor.

Chapter 49

"Have you two decided where you are going to live?" Andrea asked Coleman.

"Well, we talked about Lake City. Misti wants the autonomy of living in a new city with a new husband. She wants to start her own business there. An exercise class using pole dancing routines."

"Are you sure Lake City is ready for her? It's very conservative there, Coleman." Andrea said.

"Don't underestimate Misti. Behind that pretty face is the mind of a businessman. She'll succeed at whatever she does. Lake City has never seen anything like her and they'll be fascinated. First the honeymoon."

"Where might that be?" Trish asked joining them.

Their conversation was interrupted by the clink of glasses for a gracious toast by Lanier introducing Mr. and Mrs. Coleman Butler to the wedding guests. The band, consisting of drums, keyboard and guitar started playing
" *If You Like What You See, Put a Ring On It*" while Misti and Coleman danced together for the first time as husband and wife.

Mother and Isabelle, with help from Jackson, and the LitChix, carried platters loaded with food to the dining room table and buffet. All of the food was prepared by

Mother and looked as if it were straight off the cover of a magazine.

"Really, Mother," Andrea said. "You could start a catering business. Let's talk about that after the wedding."

"Oh, I like that idea," Mother beamed. "Something like 'Best Bet Catering Company.' You wanted me to stop using liquor in my cooking, and I have. I've found some herbs that are much better. If we bought some of those special grow lights, we could put that gloomy old basement to good use and have a regular little 'herb' greenhouse down there. Extra money for the Justice Center, you know." Mother's eyes twinkled. She hurried back into the kitchen.

Misti tip-toed behind Andrea and gave her a hug. "Thank you for everything. Everyone has been so wonderful to me. Coleman and I are going to slip out. We both hate goodbyes. When we get back from our honeymoon, we can have a good long girls' talk. I promise." She handed Andrea her little violet bouquet. "I hope you are the Justice Center's next bride." She beamed as she grabbed Coleman's arm. They hurried out the back door and into Coleman's rented limousine.

"Did Misti just leave?" Cay asked, coming back into the dining room. She saw the bouquet in Andrea's hands. "What? She's not throwing her bouquet? I feel cheated."

Andrea frowned. "That's how she wanted it. She said to thank everybody and we'll talk when she gets back. That took me by surprise. I guess we just party on. Jackson, have you eaten yet?"

"First rate," Jackson said. "Mother is some cook. I forgot to tell you something. While I was cleaning the library fireplace this morning, I noticed some burned paper in there. Tell your future residents not to put paper in the fireplace. Sometimes it goes straight up the flue and you can get a bad roof fire that way. It just takes a couple of sparks. No harm done this time."

"Misti was the one who wanted the fire last night," Andrea said, "but I'll post a little sign next to the fireplace as a reminder to anyone else. Thank you Jackson." Lanier appeared with his hand extended to lead Andrea to the dance floor.

Cay said. "Just a minute Jackson, I couldn't help but overhear your conversation. What did you do with the papers you found?"

"Put them in the dumpster. There wasn't much..."

"Jordan, to the dumpster," Cay yelled as she grabbed Jordan by the hand and pulled her through the kitchen and out the back door, nearly toppling Mother in the process. "Grab some plastic bags from the counter. Quick!"

"Oy, what's going on Cay?" Jordan stumbled as she grabbed a handful of bags. "Why are we going to the dumpster? Did you lose something valuable? Like your mind maybe?" Jordan asked, as Cay rounded the corner of the Justice Center dragging her along as quickly as she could.

"Come on, Jordan." Cay huffed. "Just help me here. Jackson said there were charred papers in the fireplace and Misti was the only one in the library last night. If Misti was burning papers, I want to know what they were." Cay tried to push up the top of the dumpster with little luck.

"How are you going to see anything even if you do get the top up?" Jordan asked. "This thing is as tall as you are. Maybe we should get Jackson's help."

"I won't ask a man to help me go 'dumpster diving.' "Cay said.

"But you'll ask me?"

"Of course. On the count of three jump and push with me, doggone it. Ok, ready? One, two, three, push! Great. I think we have it." The top flopped back with a bang. "Now, I've got to stand on something. Look around, Jordan. There's got to be something I can step on. I knew I would regret wearing heels." Jordan spotted a wooden pallet used in the apartment renovation and dragged it over.

Jordan complained. "OK. I've ruined a perfectly good manicure, I'm about to destroy my best suit, and I am going to have some nasty bruises. This better be worth it."

Cay kicked off her blue pumps, and climbed the pallet as if it were a ladder. "Well I'm going to have splinters in places I can't even mention, so stop complaining. Hold it steady, Jordan it's swaying too much." Cay threw her leg over the edge of the dark green metal bin.

"Oh, my God! You aren't getting down in that filthy dumpster, are you?" Jordan asked. "Cay, that's really disgusting." She grinned. "I'm so proud of you."

"Jackson said he found those papers this morning. There has been a lot of trash go out since then. I need a flashlight."

"Back in a flash," Jordan said. She ran back around the building and back into the kitchen. Out of breath, she gasped, "Flashlight."

"Where have you been? Jordan, you're a wreck," Trish said, as she returned an empty hors d'oeuvre tray to the kitchen. "Are you OK?"

Jordan shook her head trying to catch her breath. "Nope, no problems." She grabbed the flashlight Mother handed her, and raced back outside. She tossed the flashlight into the dumpster.

"Ow!" Cay said. "You could have shouted 'fore' or something to warn me. OK. This is better. Actually, we keep a pretty neat dumpster. I'm moving several bags to one side to see if there is any paper underneath." There was a pause and considerable grunting. Jordan could hear the rustle of trash bags.

"Nothing there. Now I'm going to move some of the bags in front." Another pause as she heard Cay tromped over the bags. Jordan heard some of them pop. "Ah, ha! This looks promising," Cay said. "This bag has some burned papers. Looks like an old records, maybe…"

"Oh great," Jordan said. "We are going to learn Misti's shame at flunking math in the sixth grade. If it doesn't get better than that, I am going to be really pissed."

"I think it does get better. A lot better. People don't burn innocuous things, only incriminating stuff," Cay said. "I am going to hand the papers to you. Be careful. Some parts are burned and about to crumble. Put them into the baggies."

Jordan climbed the pallet to reach the papers in Cay's outstretched hand. She carefully put the charred remains into baggies as Cay continued to pass them to her.

"How much more have you got? I'm getting soot all over me and I am almost out of baggies."

"OK, that's all. I'm coming out."

Chapter 50

Jordan, Cay and Trish huddled together in the oversized kitchen pantry for privacy. Trish was clearly annoyed. "Exactly why are we squished into this pantry during Misti and Coleman's wedding reception? What is so important that it can't wait?"

Cay cleared her throat. "Jackson said he threw away some charred papers this morning. It was Misti who was burning something in the fireplace last night and I want to know what it was. Jordan and I got them out of the dumpster and we think they are important enough they can't wait." Cay cleared off a shelf and began to sort the pieces of paper as if they were a puzzle.

Trish put her hands on her hips. "Cay, why are you prying into Misti's private life this way? What is the point?"

"Well, think about it, we never really identified the murderer of Lew, the thug in Piedmont Park and that man in you know who's condo. They all had wet kisses on their cheeks, male DNA, but it didn't match any known criminals. "

Jordan glared at Cay. "Why would you bring that up again and spoil my joy in my new condo?"

Cay ignored her and continued. "We assumed Misti was innocent. What if she is involved in this crime spree more than we first thought? These papers could provide some vital information."

Trish didn't try to hide her irritation. "Cay, the police are satisfied this was a drug war between rival Vegas factions. All the evidence points to the "Bunny Boy", Lew Cannon, as the Southeast drug connection. Why would we doubt the police?"

"For one thing, they've been wrong before. Without our help, Andrea would be sitting on death row right now, convicted of Sonny's murder."

"Hey, watch it," Jordan said. "Bongiovanni would have never let Andrea go to jail. He's way too cute to do that."

"Think about it, Trish," Cay wiped the perspiration off her forehead with the back of her hand leaving soot streaks behind. "Isn't this what Lanier told us to do when we had lunch at Brio? He said we were supposed to find other suspects to pin it on to clear Misti, and that's what we did."

"Hey, I kinda like where she is going with this," Jordan grinned. "There is so much we don't know about Misti. For instance, what if she used that USB key to muddy the waters and take the heat off of her." Jordan snapped her fingers. "Maybe that's exactly what she did. It doesn't even matter if everything on the key is true, just so there's enough information for the cops to verify and go off on a wild goose chase. Sort of a magician's diversion – get the audience to look at your right hand while you pull the rabbit, ouch, there is that word again, oh well, pull the rabbit out of the hat with your left."

Cay nodded. "Suppose you wanted to pull off a couple of murders, what better diversion than producing a key containing a whole encyclopedia of crimes committed by drug cartels? Maybe Misti arranged for poor Vassily or whatever that guy's name was, to get the key to her in Vegas. One of the cartels chased Vassily, which he didn't expect, and they caught him, but not before he passed the key along to Misti. The cartel then killed poor Lew by accident, probably fulfilling a contract on Misti. My best guess is that Lew was in the wrong place at the wrong time and the real target all along was Misti."

Trish said, "Wait a minute. Wouldn't these be the same guys who blew up the yoga studio? If they thought Misti would be killed in the explosion, why would they rig her bowling ball to take out Lew?"

Jordan's eyes widened. "Omigod, do you think Misti rigged that bowling ball to make it appear the cartel was after Lew and not her? One thing we know for sure, the cops would much rather have the evidence against a whole drug ring than catch just one murderer of a few low level dealers and hit men. Are you sure Misti wasn't born in Jersey? Sounds like a home girl to me."

Cay stopped sorting the charred pieces and began studying them.

Trish moved a few cans of soup and took out a Hershey's chocolate almond bar from its hiding place, unwrapped it and munched absentmindedly. She said. "So if this scenario could possibly be true, you're saying Misti swapped the key for her freedom from prosecution for the murder of Lew, which was her intent all along. The cartel took the blame for his death for sure. This is theoretical of course. Still someone did try to kill Misti when she was supposed to be in your van at Brio, Jordan, and they tried again and failed in Piedmont Park."

Cay looked up from sorting. "Do you suppose Misti killed the man in the park restroom? And what about the hit man in you-know-who's condo closet? Maybe she used her 'errand time' to clean out that drug condo before the cops saw it."

Jordan piped up. "Meanwhile, Misti walks away with a nice portfolio of art, a huge bank account and a ton of prime Atlanta real estate. Shit, I kinda admire that in a woman."

"All this speculation is making my head spin," Trish said. "I refuse to believe Misti is a heartless murderer who took advantage of us and everyone else. Cay, I never want you or Jordan on my bad side. You two are positively diabolical in your thinking. I still don't believe Misti is smart enough to pull all this off. Jordan do you really buy into Cay's theory?"

Jordan shrugged. "It makes sense in a weird kinda way."

"Here, Jordan. Help me sort these last scraps of paper on this shelf," Cay said.

"Look, this is a birth certificate. Here's a name, 'Mikel,' Jordan said. "Ooh, I like that spelling. Very Euro." She put that paper on the left. "And here is something else on the same page. 'Lapin'. Omigod, French for 'rabbit'. Remember when Isabelle found that name on the key? And she twisted it all around and got that code name? We thought that was Lew."

" Hozk," Cay replied. "M.Hozk. This is beginning to make sense. Lew's love of acrostics. That was on the key as the link to the name on the condo."

Jordan practically shouted, "Holy shit, here are some hospital records! Mikel had a sex change operation! Through the marvels of medical break-throughs, Mikel became MISTI!!"

"And my cousin married her!" Trish said putting her hand over her heart. "Oh my word. My poor Coleman."

"How do you think I feel? I am the one who married them."

Trish patted Cay's shoulder. "It certainly isn't your fault. If you hadn't performed the service, someone else would have."

Cay said, "Well, I have the license and it has to be filed at the Fulton County clerk's office within three days for the marriage to be legal. What should I do?"

Jordan said, "What if you sorta forget to file the license? This marriage is Misti's ticket to a respectable life. I think Coleman would do anything for her even if he knew the truth."

"Where exactly can they have a respectable life?" Trish asked

"I'd say just about anywhere," Cay said, "unless the cops connect the male DNA found in the kisses on Lew, the hit man in Piedmont Park and the man murdered in you-know-who's condo to Misti. Just speculating. That key and the deal exempted her from prosecution for Lew's murder only.

"Thanks," Jordan said. "I really want to keep that image in my condo fresh."

"Just putting the clues together, Jordan. It's not personal." Cay said. "The main thing we get out of piecing these burned scraps of paper together is that Misti started out life as a guy. Mikel Lapin. That 'Lapin' is the name on the USB key, so that tells me Misti could be the 'Rabbit' the key refers to, not Lew. Also, Misti could have been the brains in the drug operation." Cay stopped and took a deep breath.

Trish said. "If the police find out that Misti's DNA matches the saliva on the victims, that could be a problem. She might have started out Mikel and been surgically changed to Misti, but her DNA never changes. It will always be male."

Jordan nodded, "But Cay and I saw Misti nude. That first day she came flying in the Justice Center with the tale of Lew's murder. She sure looked like a 'she' to me."

"If she didn't look like a woman, it wouldn't have been a very successful operation, would it?" Cay said. "Besides, the Crime Scene Unit ran the saliva through their computers and got no matches for the DNA they found. They would have to take a sample of Misti's saliva and do the tests again. At this point Misti has been exonerated. Right now they are looking for other criminals who are already in their data banks. Remember, Misti has never been arrested before."

Trish frowned. "Cay, where did you get into all this deducting stuff? Not to mention your familiarity with sex-change surgery? You continue to amaze me with the breadth and weirdness of your knowledge."

"Actually this is sort of like my job. Old manuscripts are often a hunt, thinking of possibilities, not believing most of what you see or read, if the search is for something of value. It's a kind of detecting, and I worship *CSI*. Of course I could be completely wrong, and every word out of Misti's mouth could be the gospel truth."

Trish frowned, stuffing the empty Hershey wrapper in her dress pocket. "OK. Now that we have this information, what are we going to do with it? If we give it to the police, this scandal will almost certainly close the Justice Center. Poor Andrea, her dreams and investment gone before it even proved helpful to rehabilitate one abused woman. All of us believe in this project."

Cay nodded somberly. "That's heavy. I didn't think of that. I got excited finding this stuff and figuring out what it meant. I am not sure what we should do."

Jordan said, "Isabelle was the one who deciphered all that mumbo-jumbo on the key. Why don't we give these papers to her and use her analytical mind to help us decide what to do. Remember how helpful she was in solving Sonny's murder?"

Andrea's voice could be heard through the pantry door. "Chix? Where are you? The Lake City ladies want to talk with you about your book club so they can get one started in Florida."

Trish stuck her head out the door. "Andrea, we're planning a surprise in the pantry. We'll be right out, but first we have to talk to Isabelle. Isabelle? Are you still in the kitchen?"

"Here I am," said Isabelle.

Trish grabbed her arm and hustled her into the already crowded pantry.

Cay took a deep breath. "Isabelle, we need your objectivity and counsel right now. Jordan and I found charred pieces of paper which prove Misti had a sex-change operation and may be the Southeast drug contact and not Lew. She started life as a male, Mikel Lapin – the rabbit in French. She may be the one who killed all those people and Lew was just an innocent pawn."

Isabelle looked stunned.

Cay continued, "What should we do with this information? If we turn this over to Lanier or the police, this revelation could be the end of the Justice Center. The critics would have a field day with this. Misti would go to prison for murder and Coleman would be devastated."

"Where are these pieces of paper?" Isabelle frowned.

"Over here," Cay said and pointed out the pieces on the shelves.

"Hmm." Isabelle moved closer and studied them intensely. "Let's put all of them into one of the larger plastic bags."

Cay meticulously put the papers in one baggie and handed it to Isabelle. Isabelle opened the door and walked to the kitchen sink. She stared out the window for almost a minute, looked at the baggie, then glanced back at the Chix. She tightened her lips into a narrow slit and filled the baggie with water. Then she dropped the soggy contents in the disposal and turned it on.

The Chix gasped. "What the hell…" Jordan said.

Isabelle wiped her hands on a dish towel. "I cannot bear to see Andrea's noble dreams die so soon. This Justice Center will help so many unfortunate women. Besides, Misti is beginning a brand new life with a husband who adores her. 'Let sleeping dogs lie', I always say." She turned off the disposal. "All this was just circumstantial information along with a lot of imagination thrown in and doesn't prove a thing. You asked for my help and you got it. That is the mission of the Justice Center. Women helping women start over. We believe in second chances, right, Chix?" She folded the towel carefully and placed it on the counter.

Andrea opened the kitchen door and called, "Hey everybody. come on and rejoin the party." Her eyes widened as she looked at Cay and Jordan. "Cay, Jordan you two look like you've been in a mud wrestling contest. Why don't you go upstairs and get cleaned up. I've got a surprise for everyone. I hope it will start a tradition for all our weddings here at the Justice Center."

When Jordan and Cay returned a little less disheveled, Andrea collected them at the bottom of the stairs and led the way back into the entrance hall. The pink bunny ice sculpture in the middle of the dining room table was beginning to melt. "Bunny Hop," she shouted. "Everybody! Get in line!"

Epilogue

Three months later....

"Do you know the sweetest thing?" Coleman asked Misti, as she came through the front door after teaching her last pole dancing class of the day. "It's handing my sweaty sweetie a smoothie made by yours truly's loving hands. Misti took the orange concoction, sat in a soft chair and took off her sneakers. "I don't know how you can keep this place as spotless as you do and still work. You are one amazing woman."

"Coleman, you are my darlin'. How many women have a husband as wonderful as you waiting at home. I just want everything to be spotless and perfect for you. I have to admit I am a little tired tonight. We don't have plans, do we?"

"Not a thing. Nothing on TV, no reason to go out. We'll just have to stay in and enjoy home life, I guess." He sat on the arm of the chair and kissed her on top of her head.

"I know what we can do," Misti said, bouncing up enough to bump Coleman in the nose. "Ooh, sorry Baby. Did I hurt you?"

"Nothing you could do would hurt me, Sweetie pie. What did you have in mind?"

"Well, do you like doing puzzles? The crossword kind, not picture puzzles."

" I've never really paid attention to them," Coleman said, his enthusiasm level going down a notch.

"Maybe I can get you hooked on them. I am the best. Anagrams, codes, all that stuff. My brain just works that way. I tried to get Lew interested, and he tried, but he couldn't really get into it." She leaned over and gave Coleman a big kiss on the cheek.

"Here, I have a puzzle book in the drawer. I'll show you." She pulled out the end table drawer, removed a thick paperback, and thumbed through it until she found what she was looking for.

"Oh, this is a fun one," Misti said, stopping on a page covered with what looked like a web and word clues. "Two people can do it. It's called a spider and fly puzzle. See? Both people figure out the words that go on these lines, like a spider web. The spider chases the fly. You can be the fly, and I'll be the spider."

The doorbell interrupted Misti's reading of the first clue.

"You stay right where you are, Honey Bun," Coleman said. I'll get the door and be right back." A minute or two passed and Coleman returned to the living room, looking a bit paler than usual. He was followed by two serious looking men in dark suits.

"Sweetie, these men said that they are from the F.B.I. and they are looking for Misti Cannon. I told them that you were Misti Butler, Mrs. Coleman Butler, but they seem unconvinced and want to speak to you. Do you want me to stay?"

"That's all right darlin'. Why don't you wait for me in the kitchen while I talk to these nice gentlemen?"

Good idea, Precious. I'll clean up. I know how important it is to you for everything to be spotless."

Misti stood, kissed Coleman, and smiling, turned to face the two F.B.I. agents. "Now, gentlemen. What can I do for you?"

Book Club Questions

1. Relationships between women is a major theme of the LitChix series. In *Killer Condo,* new levels of friendships are explored. Discuss the friendship dynamics among the main characters.

2. What are some of the most important qualities of friendship to you?

3. Jordan's marital unhappiness leads to a lot of exploration in *Killer Condo.* Do you think a new condo, a new male relationship, and/or a new life direction provide the answers she seeks?

4. Is there a character in the book you would like to know better? Which one and why?

5. If *Killer Condo* were made into a movie who would you pick to play each of the following roles:
    A. Cay Curtis
    B. Jordan McKeehan
    C. Trish Townsend
    D. Andrea Simmons
    E. Misti Cannon
    F. Isabelle O'Brien
    G. Mother O'Brien
    H. Jackson Randall – please don't spend more than a couple of hours enjoying this particular visual

6. Do you think the concept of the Women's Justice Center is a good idea? Could it work in Atlanta, Georgia, or in your hometown? What services would you provide if you created such a center?

And coming in 2011 ....

Remember those happy days of high school? Parties at the lake, football games, your first love? What about the friends you will always remember, and the enemies you will never forget? That girl who moved into town and stole your boyfriend right out from under your nose, and married him, no less. The one who now has the stylish wardrobe, lavish home – all the things you should have had. Yep, Dede, that's her. **Dede Blaine is Dead...Again** is the third in the LitChix Murder Mystery series.

Want to name a character in **Dede Blaine is Dead...Again**? Go to www. The LitChix.com and see how you can submit the name of a friend, an enemy, or maybe your own.

Also, look for **The LitChix Cookbook: Darn Good Food That's Not Hard to Fix,** with recipes inspired by the mysteries.

To order, please visit our website: **www.TheLitChix.com**

Or write to GeorgiaAdams75@Gmail.com